I0638997

A is for Everyone

Dennis Vanderspek

A is for Everyone

Dennis Vanderspek

Winner of the 2021 Kenneth Patchen Award
for the Innovative Novel

Journal of Experimental Fiction 95

JEF Books/Depth Charge Publishing

A is for Everyone
Copyright © 2023 by Dennis Vanderspek
All Rights Reserved

Cover art and design by Carolyn Parrish
Copyright © 2023 by Carolyn Parrish
All Rights Reserved

Winner of the 2021 Kenneth Patchen Award
for the Innovative Novel

ISBN 1-884097-95-2
ISBN-13 978-1-884097-95-9
ISSN 1084-547X

This volume is volume 95 of
The Journal of Experimental Fiction

JEF

JEF Books/Depth Charge Publishing
The Foremost in Innovative Fiction
Experimentalfiction.com

JEF Books are distributed to the academic journal market by EBSCO

For Sacha and Molly

Probably a crab would be filled with a sense of personal outrage if it could hear us class it without ado or apology as a crustacean, and thus dispose of it. "I am no such thing," it would say; "I am myself, myself alone."

(William James, *The Varieties of Religious Experience*)

It is a curious feature of philological nomenclature that extended entities receive the label 'noun' when from the Second Law we know dynamic systems passing through successively higher entropic states alone constitute the phenomena marking the passage of time. Each thing is an event, a radiation.

(Alva and Aidan Perrin, "Spatial Anisotropy in Vector Fields of the Hypertriton: Preliminary Considerations")

A is for Aardvark

You're three and your mother opens a plastic book of animals and points to the first page: see? You're in a restaurant with laminated placemats for kids. You're at home and a TV is on in the living room while you toddle around with ice cream on your fingers looking outside and wondering what's in other people's back yards. What do other people look like? What do they eat? Where did they come from? If you weren't you would you be them? And in the background comes the singsong voice on the TV: *A is for aardvark, digging in the earth.*

Aardvarks must get tired of being first all the time, though. It's nice at the beginning: you get your pick of rooms on Noah's Ark and so forth. But the other animals start to resent you. There's the aardwolf right behind you, and they have teeth. Then you're in school quietly doing your sums and the teacher says let's take turns writing answers on the board. We'll go around the room alphabetically, she says. It's the only way to be fair.

A is for Abacus

An abacus is an ancient counting machine. You slide a bead for so many bolts of cloth, so many pieces of silver, so many horses, so many people. The abacus led to the computer. Between the abacus and the computer was the Difference Engine of Charles Babbage. He created a machine that would calculate precise sums by cranking a handle connected to a complex arrangement of brass gears. He wanted to keep merchants and bankers from losing money because of errors in arithmetic tables. It is not widely known that the people who made these tables were called *calculators*. Still less widely known is that Charles Babbage's mathematician friend Ada Lovelace, daughter of the English poet Lord Byron, had a dream about a machine that used symbols rather than numbers and did much more than Babbage's math—even make music. This dream was the first conceptualization of computer code.

Almost no one knows that Charles Babbage was inspired by a robot called The Turk that travelled around Europe and America for half a century beating people at chess. The Turk was a mechanical man who sat at a desk and used a metal arm to pick up and move chess pieces. Audiences were astonished. After seeing it, the idea of a thinking machine took hold of Charles Babbage.

The robot was a fake, though: underneath the machine-man a chess master pulled hidden levers to move the metal arm. He had his own small chessboard and candle inside with him and copied the game over his head as the pieces moved. Out of this deception the modern computer was born: the man-machine inside the machine-man turned gears in Charles Babbage's head while Ada Lovelace moved to Surrey, had three children, took up gambling, and dreamed of music

A is for Abandon

Abandon is either dancing happy freedom or you and your sister accidentally left behind by your parents at a rest stop outside Las Vegas. They did come back though.

A is for Abashed

A man walks into a flower store on Valentine's Day to buy roses. It's already too late but he has to try. What'll ya have she says. A dozen red roses. So she starts with the cellophane and trimming the stems and says for the wife? Yeah yeah he says because he's too happy to bother and maybe you're new around here. And in walks the wife and says oh here you are and are those for me? You shouldn't have, you shouldn't have. And the gal with the scissors stops mid-air, looks one to the other, says nothing and goes back to trimming. That's abashed.

A is for Abate

From French *abatre,* from Latin *battere,* to beat. Hence assault and battery and abattoir, the slaughterhouse. But also a summer storm as it begins to ease and the smell of ozone and petrichor, and a lingering rattle in gutters and drainpipes that turns cheerful when the sun comes out again, the way fading thunder takes on a touch of nostalgia, and people flap their umbrellas and let their dogs out, and you step off the bus and see steam rising in wisps on the sidewalk and suddenly think: I am in a busy city with cars and people and a job and rent coming due, and time and the certainty of death, but right here on the sidewalk is the miracle, this touch of sun on water that makes the world green and lets me live. And for an instant you slip sideways right there on the honking, clattering street. The rain, we would say in this case, has abated. Abate is also a sudden grateful ebbing of pain just when you can't take it anymore.

A is for Abbey

An abbey is where monks live. Tintern Abbey is a famous ruin in Wales. Monks lived there, then fire, then monks again, then a king fleeing the Black Death, then starving workers, more fire, then wild roses twisting through broken windows and rubble, then poets and painters, tourists, more tourists, then tourists with cameras. Then it became important.

A is for Abdicate

When you give up a responsibility you are said to abdicate. King Edward VIII abdicated the throne of Britain in 1936 to marry Wallis Simpson who was American and divorced. But an abdication can be small too.

My father took me to a zoo in Las Vegas once to see an aardvark. He didn't want to but I was excited for the aardvark because I thought it was an anteater and I begged and wheedled. In my mind the aardvark-anteater was connected to stories about animals who became constellations. The aardvark was my bull and ram, my lion and scorpion: I wanted to see him rise and lick up all the stars with his long tongue. But at the zoo the aardvark was only a dirt-covered donkey-eared pig-nose with a sad turnip face, and in my disappointment I blamed not the aardvark, not myself for being wrong, but my father who patiently explained what an anteater is, that they are from South America and not Africa, that the aardvark lives by rooting in the earth.

A is for Absent

When I wanted to get out of school I would lie with my head hanging over the edge of the bed and call in my mother in to see how flushed I was. My sister, two years younger and less practiced, would just pinch her cheeks hard and hope for the best. But later, years later, when she really was sick and missed almost a month of school, my mother came in one morning and asked how she was feeling, and my sister, full of fever, could only say in a whisper *I can hear my bones singing.* So she had me there.

A is for Actaeon

Actaeon was a hunter. He guarded Athens with his mighty hounds. One day he was hunting deer in the woods and came upon Artemis, the virgin goddess, bathing in a forest pool. She cursed him for seeing her naked: if he tried to speak he would turn into a stag. Actaeon heard his hounds baying in the distance and tried to call to them, but of course he was transformed instantly and the hounds heard only the bellowing of a deer. They chased Actaeon and would have torn him to pieces except that Andromeda, the raven goddess, swooped down and carried him up into the sky to live with her. If you lie outside at night you can still see them in a triangle: draw a line from Cassiopeia to Andromeda, down to The Hunter and back up. Actaeon is still there chasing her, his head a halo of fiery antlers.

A is for Adirondack

If I die, scatter my ashes on a black lake at midnight when the water's quiet and full of stars. There's a loon just on the edge of hearing or an owl, or something else otherworldly, and it's dignified and beautiful as a well-planned funeral, or like my sister's wedding on the solstice last year: they wanted an outdoor ceremony with just candles, no electricity at all, because they were like that, and when the wind picked up and the lights went out I almost cried from laughing, or laughed from crying, I forget which. It doesn't matter. What I'm saying is, if it's a night like that, just pour me straight out into the moon and walk away.

People call me morbid, but that's only because they've never known the dust. Maybe you've never known the dust either. Maybe you've never sat in a filthy Quonset hut smelling the dust of a wood duck nailed to a plastic log with outstretched dusty wings like it just flew in from a garbage dump for the breeding season. Maybe you've never sat in a kiosk half indoors and half out, the way the junk itself can't decide whether to muster the effort to exist for another decade on someone's mantel or else just kick out and molder into nothing right then and there.

Take this clock. The movement is seized but my boss, Mr Riordan, tacked a mismatched bezel to its face because he knows nobody, but nobody he says, buys old clocks to tell time. But stick it on grandma's dresser, sure. She'd love that bullet-riddled gas station sign, too; throw that in. Plus the duck. Maybe she knew that duck during the war. Maybe that duck got her out of a scrape with an enraged lover who caught her stealing his favourite cleaver, tobacco chopper, candlesticks, Mason jars of buttons, train sets, badminton rackets, framed moon landing headlines, black marble ashtrays from hotel lobbies, Firestone coasters, Crosley radios, stacks of mismatched dinner plates with faded gilt rims, trays of cutlery tied with elastic like asparagus ($2 a bunch), shoeboxes of postcards, shoeboxes of daguerreotypes and autochrome portraits of women in boats, shoeboxes of chunky plastic jewelry, claw feet from footless bathtubs, unadjustable wrenches, narcoleptic dolls in haunted prams, rusty garden tools, lightbulbs, quart-baskets of light switches, dead batteries, topographic maps, poker chips, tourist ukuleles, baseball cards that smell nothing like bubblegum, stacks of board games, puzzles, and all the other flotsam where I sit on a reclining, slatted, two-legged wooden deck chair—an Adirondack—taking money from rummagers week after week. Toss a match and go. Do it for grandma if you won't do it for me.

—How much is this basket a woman says. An urchin is lurking next to her and I note with disgust the coil of pink plastic wire that tethers it to her wrist. Animals.

—It's a trug not a basket, I tell her. A trug has slats along the bottom and sides for carrying food instead of a basket that's woven. This is a Sussex Trug. You can tell because it has brass nails and mahogany veneer along the top. Trugs were invented by Vikings you know. They'd split a log with an axe and hollow it out to carry food. Nowadays trugs are made out of willow. It's the same wood used for cricket bats.

—Oh. That's very interesting. You're very knowledgeable. Is that the price on the bottom? There's a sticker there with some writing.

—Twenty bucks.

—Oh. Ok she says and puts it down.

This happens roughly five hundred times every Saturday. I have become a connoisseur of human covetousness. I have developed an almost supernatural ability to find the hairline crack between fear and greed; it's usually turned to the wall. My mission is to uncover it. I believe I was put here, at least on weekends, to be a curator of cracks. Of course I get paid whether the junk sells or not, and if I skip movies and dating I might even be able to scrape up enough for another semester. Rent and tuition at least if I add in the scrounging jobs with the truck Mr. Riordan gives me. Truck jobs are unpredictable, but I get a better cut because he knows I have this ability. He'll always make his money.

Take last weekend. I took the truck to meet an old guy in Lakefield who was selling an organ. Now lots of old guys have organs and they're almost uniformly garbage. They learn a little piano from lessons they traded for eggs during the war, then they decide Jehovah wants them to hold down the Bossanova button and pick out "When the Saints Go Marching In" on one finger. That lasts about a month. Then the organ goes into a basement or barn until the guy dies or, as in this case, comes to the realization that $50 isn't much for a barely used organ but it'll still buy another case of Dippity-do. Then it's truck day.

I show up and of course it's all indescribably sad. The first clue is the torn lace curtain on the front door that was sewn up with dental floss during the reign of Harry Truman. Then he answers the door and I *almost* feel bad for what I'm about to do.

He leads me out to the barn, which of course is a museum of the worst things imaginable. Have you ever made chit-chat with a face of broken rakes leaning up against a cobwebbed baby's crib in a quiet barn on a scorching summer day? Those teddy bears in smiling milkpaint? The treadle sewing machine stacked with bald snow tires under a 1952 Portland Cement calendar? But there in the barn, to my surprise when he rolled it out, stood a decently preserved Hammond B2. Sure it's not a B3 but it's still a score. I even spot a Leslie parked behind a stack of crates.

While he talks I slide the drawbars in and out like an idiot to check the action. Then I tell him about my plan to gut the organ and convert it into a guitar amplifier. I do this mostly for fun, but the guy doesn't flinch. His face looked like a straw hat with no straw and no hat. So because I'm a humanitarian, after the usual back and forth I offer him twice what he'd get selling it in the paper, which is still half what Mr Riordan will take. He agreed and I got the Leslie as a throw-in after an offhand question and a joke about Gerald Ford. He seemed happy. I was happy. Somewhere in heaven Jimmy Smith was smiling. He's got the B3 though, Jimmy. No question.

Those are truck days. They don't come very often but they give me something to think about when the weather turns hot. You probably think more people come out in on nice days and stay home when it rains, but that's because you don't know the bargain hunter mind. Anyone can go out on a sunny day and get ripped off, they'll tell you; you have to beat the dummies to get the deals. So every rainy day is packed with geniuses.

Here comes another one. She's spotted the cedar chest. Lots of people spot the cedar chest. It's like a bug light. I am convinced that a substantial portion of the human population finds the idea of a cedar chest simply irresistible. They come in for a closer look and then get distracted by the cheaper junk spread over the adjacent tables. *Zap.*

This one is hard to place, though. She's mid twenties and wearing boots that make her willowy and clompy at the same time, and a punkish band shirt I've never heard of, and she has a tattoo on her ankle and expensive-looking sunglasses clearly worn to hide rather than protect her eyes. And she's alone at a dusty, run-down, half-deserted rural flea market on a scorching Saturday afternoon. Because none of this adds up, and because I must have order in my kiosk at the center of the universe, I summon her singles ad to my mind. If you've never done this, it's a great way to get to know someone you'll never meet. Hers goes like this:

Probably unattached female, 24ish, seeks partner. Must be free spirited but willing to settle whenever I'm ready. You are attracted to tall women with a taste for knock knock jokes with an existential edge and a tattoo of a lithium atom on her right ankle. You love learning but hated school. You love small towns but couldn't wait to get out. You regard lottery tickets as investments. You have scars you can't explain and scars you can but no one asks. You secretly do not believe in God but even more secretly do. You love obscure postpunk electro, golden retrievers, tomato sandwiches, gateway drugs and gateways. People say you're smart and you have a hard time believing you don't care what they think. There are three places you call home, one of which exists only in your imagination. You'd like to visit the Azores someday just for the sound but you're counting on not living that long. You're a mystery even to your friends but also dangerously honest. I'm nothing like you but nothing will be like us. References available upon request. Recent picture a plus. Smokers welcome.

She looks at the cedar chest, opens the lid, and lets it drop with a bang. She does this with a kind of elegant simplicity: let the cedars fall where they fall. Then she turns toward the miscellany spread out on the table in front of my chair. *Gotcha.*

—What are these?

—Ah. Those are actually *ceramic pet urns.* Someone had a collection I guess and it wound up here. I've never seen so many together though.

—Pet urns?

—Yep. Like, for dogs and cats. Mostly cats though I think. People find it harder to let go of cats than dogs for some reason. I have no idea. I like dogs.

—That's really sad she says with a look over her sunglasses that makes me uncomfortable.

—There's a whole industry devoted to it, I tell her. Pet urns are big business. People want to feel close to their pets after they're gone I suppose. I don't know. So they keep the urns. Then the people die and someone inherits the urns who didn't know the cats or dogs or maybe knew the person but not well enough to care, you know, to respect the deceased's final wishes regarding the disposition of said ashes and so on and so forth. I don't know where these came from though. I just sell them.

—That's alright, she said. Some of them are very beautiful. Like little jewel boxes full of memories.

—Five bucks, I said.

Her hand drifted, touching each urn separately as if she were blind.

—I'll take them all she said after a moment.

—Sure thing I said.

I removed the lid of each urn to wrap it separately in newspaper, to prevent breakage. Some of the urns were dirty or dusty, and while my hands were hidden below the table I cunningly buffed their sides on my sleeve.

A is for Advice

If you find yourself human and far from help, consider one or more of the following survival strategies, as applicable:

1. Back away slowly.
2. Eat a little and see how it goes.
3. Pull a blanket over your head and wait.
4. Walk away at a natural pace. Do not look over your shoulder. Do not whistle.
5. If caught outside during a thunderstorm, count the seconds between flash and thunder. Count out loud as though to a child. Do not attempt if a child is actually present.
6. If experiencing acute pain you may see an unblinking eye when you try to sleep. Imagine talking to your favourite birds until the eye closes.
7. If a nuthatch approaches you upside down and speaks, follow its instructions to the letter.
8. If attempting to build a fire in the rain, or if your friends have forgotten your birthday, roll wet matches in your hair until static electricity dries them out.
9. If attempting to signal a rescue helicopter by trampling letters in snow, the international symbol for travelers in distress is a square. Recall this with laughter if you want to live.

10. If government troops are suppressing ornithologists in your area, hide under the stairs. This action is recommended regardless of occupation.
11. If attempting to signal a rescue ship while lost at sea, use your underwear and a stiff pole to fashion a signaling device: pole-right for dashes and pole-left for dots. Only underwear should be used for this purpose.
12. In cases of accidental poisoning, or if someone asks you to organize any type of reunion, a mixture of tea and charcoal should be given immediately.
13. If lost in the mountains of western China, Solomon's Seal (*Disporopsis pernyi*) can be identified by its bright green lanceolate leaves and blue-black berries. The berries are poisonous, but the roots may be infused with hot water to make an effective treatment for hemorrhoids.
14. Petting caterpillars should be avoided in survival situations, but if you must, stroke front to back to avoid painful spines.
15. Wild fungi have many uses. *Armillarea mellea* tastes like honey. A giant puffball makes both an effective pillow and a passable field dressing. If death is unavoidable, look for a Chanterelle, a beautiful mushroom shaped like your mother's tulips that smells like apricots.

A is for Afterlife

Whenever Barbie died we buried her in the loose soil behind the garage, the only spot in the yard invisible from the kitchen window. Barbie didn't die very often, but when she did we buried her solemnly and with adherence to all the rites, though we changed them every time. Wooden boxes left over from bottles of Christmas wine made the best coffins. We would lie Barbie out in her summer dress and put her favourite accessories next to her, then slide the long lid up through its groove, say a prayer, and heap up the earth. My mother, weeding, would find the boxes sometimes weeks later and silently resurrect her.

A is for Alamogordo

Alamogordo is the saddest town in the saddest state in America. After leaving Las Vegas we lived there for a month while my mother got sadder and sadder.

Every house in Alamogordo has a chain link fence to keep its patch of sun-blasted desert separate from the next house's patch of sun-blasted desert. The streets are wide and everyone drives a truck. The trucks look small and sad on the giant streets, as though they knew they were meant for better things but couldn't help being born in Alamogordo.

On New York Street, near what passes for downtown, there is a tobacco shop called *The Smoker's Nook*. On the sidewalk outside stands the last and saddest cigar store Indian in America. To be last of anything is sad enough, but the wood of this particular statue had absorbed the statue's feet as if in disappointment for fifty years growing wild in the sun just to advertise tobacco products to the insensitive smokers of Alamogordo. The sculptor had carved the fingers in crude vertical slabs like a three-year-old's drawing, with the wooden cigars sticking up like a poker hand of dynamite. Looking west, past the downtown, beyond Alamogordo itself, the cigar store Indian's wooden eyes look toward the White Sands National Monument and Missile Range stretching to the San Andres mountains shimmering like a mirage over the blinding desert. It was sixty-seven miles above White Sands that fruit flies launched aboard a captured German V2 rocket became the first terrestrial creatures in space. If I could move, the cigar store Indian thinks, what would it be like to walk across all that burning sand. If I could walk just once, he thinks, what would it be like.

A is for Album

My mother stored pictures in shoeboxes on a shelf in her closet and periodically sorted them into piles for adding to scrapbooks. The pictures not worth a scrapbook she bundled with string or tucked into manila envelopes with a date and scribbled explanation before committing them to banker boxes stacked on shelves in the garage to keep them off the floor. These were photographs, I should have said: everything was kept. Film was too expensive to throw out even the ugly pictures, the flashed-out, red eyes, looking-the-other-way sort of pictures. Every awkward birthday was saved, every say-cheese family portrait and rabbit-ears prank with grinning cousins. Every wedding, graduation, bridal shower, birthday, birth and funeral was sorted in its turn. I remember my mother's hands touching each photograph deliberately as she judged their fates, as though she trusted her eyes to tell only half the story. Her entire collection would fit on a thumb drive now, but I only keep the safe pictures. Everyone only keeps the safe pictures now.

A is for Alimony

Alimony is a payment made by one spouse to a former spouse after a divorce. It derives from a Latin word meaning flourishing, healthy, because alimony was meant to provide for children when there was only one income. The Latin is *alimonia*: support, nourishment.

Down the street from where we used to live, a man was out jogging.

On the street lived another man who was divorcing his wife. The divorce was not going well and the second man had decided to kill himself and murder his wife and her lawyer all at the same time. He arranged for the final divorce papers to be signed at the house they had bought when they married. Before they arrived, however, he entered the house and disconnected the water heater. The house filled with gas. His plan was to ignite the gas with a cigarette lighter during the signing of the papers and send them all up into the sky together. In this way his wife and the lawyer would be repaid. But something went wrong and the gas ignited while he was still waiting. He was at the center of the explosion and survived, but the house was blown to bits as if by a bomb.

The jogging man was right in front of the exploding house when its garage door rocketed past his face and tore off part of the roof of another house across the street. Glass splinters raced toward him in a razor hurricane. He would have been shredded down to his Nikes except that at that very moment, between a foot in mid-air and the heel touching the road, he was shielded by the trunk of a 30-year-old linden tree growing on the front lawn of the house. The tree perfectly eclipsed the explosion at the instant the man was vulnerable, like stories of atom bomb survivors who bent down to tie a shoe behind a wall and straightened into a world of shadows. The linden tree took this world into its bark to save the man.

The jogger was 56. He was running for his health because his doctor told him he was getting paunchy. He liked to run on this street because he had lived there with his wife before they divorced. He had, in fact, lived in the very same house that now flowed around him in a river of fire and glass, and had planted the linden on the occasion of the birth of his son. His wife had bought the tree as a sapling at a local garden centre, because they were on sale and because when she saw it she remembered a linden grew outside his bedroom window at his parents' house when he was a kid. Their son had struggled with the divorce at first but went on to a thriving career as a podiatrist. The jogger still saw his son at his grandkids' birthdays, and just that Christmas he'd had a card from his ex-wife for the first time in years.

A is for Allegory

Once upon a time in Russia long ago foxes lived in towns and villages just like you and I. Some were hunters, woodcutters, or fishermen casting nets on the great rivers—because foxes, as everyone knows, are extremely clever and always thinking up new ways to keep warm or to catch their dinner.

In one village lived a forester and his wife, and they had three daughters: Anna, Donya, and the eldest, Sophia. Sophia was known far and wide as the cleverest member of the cleverest family of, as I said, one of the cleverest creatures ever to walk the earth. She was skilled in building and forging and especially in making useful things out of copper and glass, like clocks and pocket-watches, or even magical things like self-fetching slippers or a pen that when you were stuck on a crossword puffed out helpful suggestions from its top in black smoke, and you only needed to poke the word you wanted and the pen wrote it down for you. People brought their broken clocks for her to fix and she was loved by all for her kindness and skill.

Sophia's favourite place, other than her workshop, was her garden in a grove of oaks at the heart of the village. She would leave her shop at the end of the day covered in soot and bits of brass or gold or whatever she was working with and make her way through the streets to the grove. The people would see her, and because they loved her they called her *pastushka derev'yev*, the shepherdess of the trees.

But the lives of silver foxes are short and hard, then as now, and two winters came in which the river froze and the mice the foxes depended upon for food could not be found. The forester and his wife had laid in a store, but plainly another such winter would be their end. So it was that, in the way of things of that long-ago time, the two youngest daughters were married to red and white foxes who came courting from the south in rowboats as soon as the river was clear.

Sophia missed her younger sisters but kept busy in her workshop and garden. And soon enough, because that too is the way of things, she began receiving letters from her sisters about the families they had started and the warm southern lands running with mice, and a river that hardly ever froze, and could she come for a visit?

Now, Sophia, because she was very good and very kind, was happy for her sisters. She worried, however, about her parents and how they would manage if she went away herself. The thought gnawed at her and kept her awake at night. There ought to be a solution, she thought, but what it was she could not imagine. Years went by and she became withdrawn and quiet, and people began to whisper that she was consumed with envy for her sisters, or that being alone had affected her mind, and other stupid things.

One drizzly spring day Sophia left her workshop in a weary daze, still wearing her leather apron, and crossed the street to the path that would bring her to the garden in the circle of oaks. The day was too wet and cold for most and she walked alone past the market, now closed, and the village's clock tower, whose bezel had come loose and swung from one hinge. A numb melancholy seemed to soak out of the misty drizzle, and once inside the grove she walked slowly around the beds and with her eyes followed the drooping faces of young fawn-lily down to the newly turned but already weedy earth.

Suddenly she burst out weeping. Turning her face to the sky she gave her tears to the rain and said aloud: "I didn't ask to be here but I'm afraid to leave. What am I supposed to do?" And because there was only the chill air and drizzly mist, she covered her face with her paws and stood still a while. Then she knelt on one of the beds, and placing her forepaws on the ground dug her claws into the soil and let all of her unhappiness and loneliness pour down her arms and out into the old earth.

At once the circle of oaks began to tremble in every leaf, and loose sticks and twigs jumped into the air and spun like propellers. A light like the glint of dawn or the last touch of sunset flashed through the grove and the air jumped with crackling sparks. A scorching gust burst out of the ground and became a whirlwind that hummed like a hive of gigantic bees. Sophia was knocked backward and landed flat on her tail.

When she opened her eyes and stood and looked around, and shook a twig or two out of her ears, what did she see? Standing in front of her at the centre of the circle of oaks, as calm as you please, stood a grey rat and a red squirrel. The rat and squirrel looked at her with shining eyes that, if you looked closely, whirled with tiny glittering gears of copper and brass. Sophia stared in amazement.

And, as she soon discovered, the pair were amazing indeed: the rat could catch two dozen mice in an hour, quick and silent as a knife, and the squirrel could chew through more wood in two hours than a dozen young foxes swinging the finest axes. In no time the village fires were burning brightly and every fox who wanted it could have mouse pie for supper, mice on toast, steamed mice, boiled mice, or mice in tins for those who didn't feel like cooking. Foxes who got tired of mice taught the rat to fetch other things as well, and the squirrel would accomplish any task almost as fast as you could say it. Both were soon a familiar sight all over the village.

"What shall I call you?" Sophia asked them one day. But they made no answer and only looked back at her with shining eyes.

By summer the village had become a thriving town, then by fall a busy city. The foxes lived in tall tree trunks hollowed out by the squirrel, so that on a bright winter afternoon you might see a thousand pointy fox-faces smiling down at you from a thousand tidy balconies. It no longer seemed important to know how to hunt or manage wood, or how to hop across the river-ice when it broke up in spring.

This continued until, because the way of things has no end, Sophia was at last quite old. Her parents were long gone and her sisters and nephews and nieces had all forgotten about her. None of the city foxes brought clocks for her to fix anymore or asked for help with their gardens. She lived alone in a small apartment over her old workshop, now closed and boarded, and the weeks and months blended together.

Finally, after a long decline, the time came for Sophia to die. And as she lay with her breath coming shorter and shorter, lo, the rat and squirrel appeared again and stood next to her bed. She had not seen them in many years. They looked at her with blank expressions and said "mother, what will we do?" But Sophia only whispered *pastushka derev'yev* over and over. And then she died.

The rat and squirrel disappeared from the village. Without them, the foxes immediately began to quarrel over food and fuel. The quarrelling soon turned into fighting, and the city divided into increasingly belligerent factions. Finally, the bitter war of the foxes began. When it was over the towers had been thrown down, the balconies were smashed, and the people were destroyed or scattered. So ended the great city of the foxes.

The tale, however, is not quite ended, for when the last fire had burned out, lo, the rat and squirrel appeared again. Quickly and silently they went up and down the streets of the ruined city collecting the fox bones and fox skulls and fox fur of the unburied dead and carrying them to the garden at the centre of the circle of oaks. There they heaped the bones and fur into a mound and layered on hot charcoal, then dry fir boughs, green branches of linden and tamarack, and finally a thick layer of damp moss, until the pile began to crackle and send up a pillar of steam and smoke. Then the rat and squirrel joined hands and sang a song of making and of the world's beginning and end; and as they sang, sheets of flame swept up out of the ground and folded upon itself in the shape of a fiery seed towering over their heads, until the mound had been utterly consumed. And when the singing ended and the air cleared, lo, there stood Sophia young and whole again, smiling at the rat and squirrel with shining eyes of glass and gold. And the three of them laughed and joined hands and kissed each other, and vanished forever from the world of men.

A is for Alphabet

MIKE YANKEE FOXTROT ALPHA TANGO HOTEL ECHO ROMEO WHISKEY ALPHA INDIA TANGO SIERRA WHISKEY ECHO QUEBEC DELTA WHISKEY ALPHA INDIA TANGO FOXTROT OSCAR ROMEO TANGO HOTEL ECHO CHARLIE OSCAR DELTA ECHO TANGO HOTEL ECHO KILO ECHO YANKEE HOTEL ECHO FOXTROT LIMA INDIA ECHO SIERRA UNIFORM NOVEMBER DELTA ECHO ROMEO GOLF ROMEO OSCAR UNIFORM NOVEMBER DELTA HOTEL OSCAR UNIFORM ROMEO SIERRA TANGO GOLF SIERRA DELTA ALPHA YANKEE SIERRA WHISKEY ECHO ECHO

KILO SIERRA INDIA WHISKEY ALPHA INDIA TANGO
FOXTROT OSCAR ROMEO HOTEL OSCAR MIKE ECHO
ALPHA GOLF ALPHA INDIA NOVEMBER TANGO HOTEL
ECHO NOVEMBER DELTA ROMEO INDIA VICTOR INDIA
NOVEMBER GOLF ALPHA TANGO NOVEMBER INDIA GOLF
HOTEL TANGO MIKE OSCAR NOVEMBER TANGO ALPHA
NOVEMBER ALPHA DELTA ALPHA KILO OSCAR TANGO
ALPHA WHISKEY YANKEE OSCAR MIKE INDIA NOVEMBER
GOLF WHISKEY ECHO PAPA LIMA ALPHA YANKEE VICTOR
DELTA NOVEMBER TANGO HOTEL ECHO LIMA ECHO
TANGO TANGO ECHO ROMEO GOLF ALPHA MIKE ECHO
ALPHA LIMA OSCAR NOVEMBER ECHO LIMA INDIA
CHARLIE ECHO NOVEMBER CHARLIE ECHO PAPA LIMA
ALPHA TANGO ECHO SIERRA OSCAR NOVEMBER TANGO
HOTEL ECHO HOTEL INDIA GOLF HOTEL WHISKEY ALPHA
YANKEE TANGO OSCAR WHISKEY ALPHA INDIA TANGO
UNIFORM NOVEMBER DELTA ECHO ROMEO GOLF ROMEO
OSCAR UNIFORM NOVEMBER DELTA ROMEO NOVEMBER
FOXTROT ALPHA GOLF ALPHA INDIA NOVEMBER
FOXTROT OSCAR ROMEO TANGO HOTEL ECHO KILO
ECHO YANKEE TANGO HOTEL ECHO CHARLIE OSCAR
DELTA ECHO TANGO OSCAR BRAVO ROMEO INDIA
NOVEMBER GOLF UNIFORM SIERRA HOTEL OSCAR MIKE
ECHO UNIFORM TANGO ALPHA

A is for Aluminum

Crushing steel beer cans was impressive. Then aluminum cans
appeared and teenagers started balling them in one hand like paper.
These would melt in a campfire.

My parents took us camping once when they were fighting. I don't remember if they were fighting because we were camping or camping because they were fighting, but my mother took up smoking again right there around the campfire just to aggravate my father, who couldn't smoke anymore, so he drank beer and threw the empty cans on the fire and piled wood higher than anyone needed, until sparks flew into the treetops like the Fourth of July. Then out of the corner of my eye I saw it: a rivulet of aluminum trickling between two rocks like mercury, running into a flat pool and quivering like something just born into the world, shivering and quivering like something new.

A is for Anacoluthon

Carolyn Parrish was a cat but she was also a Manx, which if you do not know is the very best cat to be. Her boyfriend, Daniel, was just an ordinary Tom but he was kind to her and didn't mention her tail even once. He waited for her, too, while she finished art school and struggled to launch a career as an illustrator of children's books. Many a random Burmese might not have looked back at a crumbling apartment over a boarded framing shop in Roncesvalles with paint and broken pastels scattered over the floor and unfinished charcoal sketches sprouting from nooks like bad memories. Many a Shorthair in his tiger prime wouldn't be so patient with her bouts of despair and self-doubt. He was on the whole a good cat, that Daniel, and loyal, for a cat. And there was also, Carolyn had to admit, the grooming. Daniel had only one ear and frequently came home covered in blood and dirt, but he groomed like no cat she'd ever known. The fleas never stood a chance. So on the whole it suited Carolyn Parrish for that time to be a Manx in love.

One day she was in the kitchen feeding Julius Caesar scraps of wilted lettuce when Daniel came padding in. He was wearing the sunglasses he wore to make people think he was walking his seeing-eye rat, or sometimes to hide a bloody eye or swollen cheek. He tilted his head as he looked at he, and the sunglasses slipped off his missing ear and clattered to the floor. His eyes were round with annoyance. Carolyn stared back at him.

—Well?

—Well. So I talked to him. No dice. He has our security deposit and first and last and he's keeping it thank you very much. No chance to break the lease before spring. The bastard. Never ask a Persian for a favour.

—That's racist. And we're obviously in the wrong. What did he say exactly?

Daniel sidled in and sat near the table. His long striped tail flopped slowly side to side, measuring his agitation in precise thumps.

—Just that. He says it's mid-winter etcetera and nobody's renting and so on. He knows someone, Luna or something equally ridiculous, who might but after all maybe not and so forth. Well. So now it looks like we have no choice. There's a train leaving at six. I checked. I already talked to Jack at the station. He'll be waiting for us.

—You know I can't just leave. What about the kids?

—They're not ours! And it barely pays!

—But who looks after them? I can't just take off. I have responsibilities even if you don't.

Daniel sighed. He stood and paced in slow circles, then sat and wiped his face with the back of a paw; shook his head; licked one shoulder, then the other. Stared into a corner. Blinked. Stared some more.

The phone rang. Carolyn picked it up.

—Hello? Yes. OK. Oh? Yes. Really though? If you can that'd be. I know it's a lot. Right. But you know you don't— OK. Well, I don't know what to say, Jack. You're a lifesaver. I'll tell him. Come see us if you can. I know. I will. You too. Bye.

Hanging up the phone and turning to Daniel, Carolyn let out a long sigh of mingled relief, resignation, and anticipation. They stared at each other without speaking for a full minute.

—OK, she said at last, it seems we're free after all.

An hour later, a cold and snowy dusk was settling over Ossington and Carolyn and Daniel were trotting single-file atop a roofless, crumbling brick wall near the Spadina overpass on the way to Union Station. A wind from the frozen lake whirled fresh flakes of icy snow into their eyes and whiskers. Carolyn noticed the change first.

—It's going to snow, she said.

—It *is* snowing.

—You know what I mean.

A red and black streetcar clanked and shuddered down Ossington. On the sidewalk some children were walking home from school. A boy in a green jacket saw two cats walking on a ruined wall high over his head and scooped slushy blue-stained snow from the windshield of a parked car. Taking careless aim, he hurled a snowball with all his strength. The snowball exploded on the brick just below Carolyn and Daniel. They looked down. The boy was looking up and pointing, his mouth a red oval.

—Let's go down here, Carolyn said. It's not much further anyway. We can take the tunnels.

They jumped down from the wall and entered the Ruin.

If you're not a cat you won't know the Ruin—you've only have seen a sooty, burned-out brick shell next to a gloomy railyard, which indeed it was. But the Ruin was also a market, theatre, school, and, occasionally, as during winter storms, community shelter. Not seeing anyone, and with a labyrinth of jumbled steel and shattered archways twisting the thickening snow into needling gusts that made them squint, Carolyn and Daniel turned at a particular leaning post and made their scrambling way steadily down, down, over and through rusty machinery and piles of broken brick and rubble and slippery coal, toward the inner core of the Ruin and the high-walled rock-crusher that everyone called the Citadel. It was there they expected to meet Mr. Universe and the Grey Nebelung.

Carolyn was worried. Just spotting the gate would be difficult, and then there was still the watchword. The Ruin might be a local hub, but except in a crisis worse than any snowstorm no one entered the Citadel except by invitation. She had no way of knowing that the silver-tipped, grey-ruffed Maine Coon, whose mighty upraised paw should have challenged them for the watchword, had already left his post for the comparative comfort of the Citadel.

Before very long, however, they found the heavy green gate and pulled it up on its freezing chains. Tripping over a broken sign just inside, they set off down a well-worn path into the Citadel. The gate slid shut behind them with a clang.

Walking behind Daniel, almost blind in the dim light, it occurred to Carolyn that they were in what her mother used to call *a spot*. She had never been inside the Citadel, and she was vaguely aware of some unpleasantness that had transpired between Daniel and the Citadel's current leader. Even if they weren't stopped by Mr. Universe, and even if they met the Grey Nebelung and somehow convinced him to help them, the least unpleasant outcome was missing their train and, in a day or two, finding themselves back on cold, wet streets among schoolchildren. Carolyn shuddered.

—Daniel, she said.

—Hm? He looked over his shoulder.

—What are we doing?

—We are fleeing hardship and bad luck to begin a new life in Welcome, theoretically an hour north by train. We are walking through a cold, damp tunnel that smells like an old mousetrap and is too narrow for us to walk side by side. That is all.

—No, doing *here*. I doubt they'll just, you know, *take us in*. I don't know anyone here anymore, not that I ever really did. How about you?

—No. Maybe. I don't know. Anyhow it's better than getting pelted with snowballs. No one was guarding the gate. Maybe that's a good sign.

—Maybe.

After a few minutes trotting steadily down, a warm breeze began rising from deeper in the tunnel and wafted into their faces, both melting their whiskers and, suddenly, bringing them to a jolting stop with their hearts pounding and their ears swivelled sideways in alarm. From somewhere just ahead the unmistakable stench of dog was rising: dog and fresh blood. They looked at each other with almond pupils, then plucked up their courage and padded as stealthily as they could toward a yellow glow.

Rounding a corner, they stumbled into a bright courtroom crowded with noisy cats rushing left and right in robes and spectacles and tattered wigs. Behind a low partition, several shabby Torties and Torbies in dirty waistcoats, evidently spectators, were brawling for no apparent reason; one of the collared bailiffs hissed at them threateningly. Overhead, three candles stood at the ends of three vanes of a broken ceiling fan. On the far side of the room a pair of huge oil lamps flanked a high bench of polished wood. And in the middle of the room, in an empty space in front of the bench, muzzled, manacled, menacing, gigantic, the very picture of horror, a German Shepherd sat chained neck, chest, and foot to an iron ring set in the concrete floor. The beast was enormous, its coat a black and tan lion's mane, though filthy now and matted with blood. Even weighed down with chains the dog towered over the clerk, defense, witnesses, and prosecution. Its face was almost hidden by a sooty leather muzzle, but in its one visible eye Carolyn seemed to see a black tunnel receding into an alien and incomprehensibly violent will. The beast tugged periodically at the anchoring chain, and the shock of its strength shuddered through every Manx, tabby, and Siamese in the room.

—Well this is interesting, said Daniel.

—Wisht! hissed one of the greyhairs.

Emerging from his curtained chamber on the far side of the room, a grey, shaggy, flat-faced, notch-eared, stout-bodied British Shorthair in black robes appeared and seated himself at a tall chair behind the bench. He banged his gavel slowly three times and a bailiff in red and gold stepped forward and declaimed: *Gratiae veritas naturae, gloriosus et liber.* This court of common law is now in session!

The judge was, to their surprise, none other than the Grey Nebelung himself. Carolyn started and jabbed Daniel in the ribs with a single extended claw.

—Ow! Yes I see.

—King and judge!

—I see that too.

—We're doomed.

—Yes. Let's find a better place to sit.

They edged toward the back of the courtroom and found a spot on a bench between a Shaded Cameo and a sepia Burmese.

—Hello, Carolyn said.

—Sssht! chewed the Burmese around an enormous cigar.

The hubbub drifted down. The judge raised his gavel and then, to a convincing hush, laid it on the bench. He turned his green eyes slowly left and right. When the room had held silent for a full minute, excepting the monster's rasping breath, he spoke.

—My friends, he said, many was the time that I, just attained to the first bloom of youth, my whiskers not yet fully grown, travelled from the Ruin to the shore and back again on summer days and autumn nights, or even, as now, on winter evenings of ice and snow. And in all that time—and I am more than likely speaking now to some few only who remember those days—in all that time we knew, as taught us by our mothers and fathers, bless their memories, that the last house on the main street, the white house with a pine tree and a crooked gate, was a place of danger, and even, for many of my contemporaries, of sudden and horrible death. It was known, and we remember still the words we were taught: the path, the gate, the tiger.

A tremble ran through the court. They remembered.

—That was so long ago it seemed the thing must surely have expended what it called its life and left us in peace. And for a time there *was* peace: the gate hung on its hinges, there was no whistle or jangle of leash, no clatter of bowl. We dared hope. Some of us dared skirt the very path. Then the nightmare so long held off with discretion and counsel, and perhaps, indeed, as it now seems, with no small measure of overconfidence, was renewed. And now, at the end of an extraordinary day, the nightmare sits awaiting our judgement.

—My lord, the bailiff whispered to the judge, perhaps we should recognize—

—I was coming to that Oscar! What my bailiff here means is that we should acknowledge the tremendous sacrifice that made this moment possible. In the name of those fallen heroes and wounded, the court hereby reaffirms its commitment to justice—not revenge, not retribution—in keeping with the law and our traditional standards of evidence and truth.

A murmur rippled forward from the back rows. Many had come for quite another reason and didn't care for this talk of justice and truth. Dressed in black in the front row, widows and widowers of the recent dead shuffled uneasily. One burst into fresh tears.

The judge ignored them. Summoning to the bench the lawyers for prosecution and defense, he solemnly charged them with the duties of their offices. Then, as one, the judge, lawyers, and clerks rose and bowed to a tattered flag in the corner. The trial had begun.

The prosecution stepped forward. She was a tall, smooth Abyssinian with burnished gold eyes and tall mousy ears that might have been comical without her dignified air of confident composure.

—My god, Carolyn whispered into Daniel's good ear, that's Kitty Hawkins!

—Are you sure? said Daniel. Didn't you go to school with her?

—Yes. *And* looked after her kittens while she went through law school. I hope she loses. I could tell you some stories.

—That bad huh? Bad enough to set that thing loose?

—Maybe. It was a long time ago. She's no friend of mine though I can tell you.

—Well that's both of us done then. If himself spots me I'll be in that dog's bowl. I never told you this, Care, but, you know, you talk about your bad blood, I once—

—Shh!

Mr. Universe had fixed them with his jade eyes. He was guarding the tunnel mouth; his imposing form blocked the exit.

Kitty Hawkins walked to the middle of the courtroom and stood in front of the dripping muzzle. The creature's nostrils blew straight down into her ears. Unconcerned, she drew up her graceful neck and addressed the room in a calm and smooth voice.

—Your honour, she said, the fact of the matter is that I have no case to make. I offer my apologies. But no words are necessary to prosecute this case, not even the words one might expect in a courtroom: charges and evidence, accounts of witnesses, impact statements, expert testimony, and so on. Many of you no doubt came expecting these things. Some of you may even believe there is an unsettled point of law at issue. You are mistaken. The evidence is obvious, the crime self-evident. The accusers are here in the front row. The accused has no character to witness, and the impact is our collective history of blood, pain, and fear. You heard the judge speak rather grandly just now about long years of peace. So it was. I remember it, some of it. Some will remember more. But the salient and undeniable fact is that this creature has murdered us for as long as anyone can remember. I take no pleasure in my role as prosecutor, but I fulfil it willingly on behalf of the voiceless who will come after. I raised nine kittens on my own in little more than a shoebox full of tissue paper and never had reason to complain. I watched them grow up just as you watched yours, Charlie Parkhurst—and how many did you lose before their time? And you, Mr. Parsifal Santorini, how many of yours? And the twins here, Pelles and Oberon, where are your parents now? And you, Princess Luna? You've buried more than anyone.

My friends, I have no gift for oratory, no subtle argument to expound, no analysis of motive or clever psychological insight. The motive is obvious and psychology is impossible: the beast has no mind. Who has not known loss and yearned to know its cause? Here it sits. Chained, it is true, but alive and breathing our air, perhaps soon eating our food and enjoying the same life that just today was cut short for—how many? What is a number? I call on you in the name of the very justice so recently and elegantly praised to resolve swiftly upon the remedy prescribed under law: the creature must die.

She bowed gracefully and withdrew to the prosecution's box. The defense stepped forward. More accurately, the defense leaped to the floor from atop a filing cabinet next to the tattered flag. He was a young Devon Rex with shaggy auburn hair and almost transparent ears; his eyes were the colour of the North Atlantic and his black-tipped tail swayed back and forth with a mischievous will of its own. He collected himself, and walking boldly toward the dog stepped right under the ghastly muzzle, reeking of death and gore, as it dipped to smell him in cracking snorts like a surfacing whale, until it nearly touched the top of his head.

—Dog, he said in a loud and clear voice, what is your name?

A gasp ran through the courtroom. The prosecution sprang to her paws, her eyes indignant slits.

—Oh, do not worry my friends, do not worry, the Devon said genially to the room, as if he had just performed a card trick for a party of kittens. Then he turned and addressed the accused in a shout.

—DOG! MY NAME IS OLIVER! WHAT ARE YOU CALLED?

The muzzle oozed saliva streaked with blood. The black pit rolled.

—You see, my friends, Oliver said, backing up a few paces and facing the audience, he does not speak. Honestly, I'm not certain he *can* speak, with or without a muzzle. What do I know about dogs? I've never had a Bedlington over for tea. I've never chatted up a beagle of a summer afternoon. I've never even *stood* this close to a live dog. Running away, sure. Being chased, sure.

He paced back and forth before the judge's bench, his voice growing in confidence. As he spoke his tail flicked and coiled in a kind of spontaneous punctuation.

—I'll say this though. This dog, the one we're looking at? He *does* have a name, same as you and I. It's hanging from his collar right here—see? He pointed an outstretched paw. You hear that, dog? You have a name, just like a real person! It's "Buddy." It's right there on your tag if you can read. Now who's a good boy?

31

Buddy lunged at Oliver. The chains clanked and held. Mr. Universe observed coolly.

—Now, friends, I may guess what you're thinking: *no, he is not a good boy.* But I remind the court that we are not here not to arbitrate good and evil. Our remit is to identify unlawful acts and apply appropriate legal remedies, nothing more and I assure you nothing less.

He walked around the creature, discretely avoiding the scratched tail and bloody chains. He approached the gallery and paused, and it seemed to Carolyn that under the Rex's confidence some doubt kept rising in his eye and flicking out through his tail. Feeling a twinge of sympathy, she glanced sideways at Daniel: he was rapt. Of course, this sort of thing would fascinate him. Then she looked around the courtroom and saw the same expression on dozens of faces.

Oliver turned to the line of widows. His tone became conciliatory.

—We all know the First Law: *kill only when necessary.*

Buddy's head drooped.

—But while we're congratulating ourselves on our civility, let us also recall how we got here. No, not *here* here, where we live in relative safety and comfort under a wise and just ruler, long may he reign. No, I mean hold up your paws and look at them. Go on, look! Do it now!

Daniel shot Carolyn a quizzical look, but she was already looking down at her upturned right paw, as most were, even the Burmese, who had extracted the cigar from his mouth to do so, so that his head seemed wrapped in a smoky bonnet.

—What do you see? Seven pads: carpal, digital, metacarpal. Those help you hunt without being heard. Atop the front pads are your claws. Some of you, ahem, may have your claws partially or even fully extended right now. There's no need for embarrassment; it's only partly under your control. Between each claw and each *middle phalanx*, or toe, there's a stretchy ligament that joins the claw to the *distal phalanx*, or the front of each toe. That ligament listens to your thoughts, as one might listen to the ocean through a seashell. And when it hears you getting excited—perhaps a careless mole has popped out of a tunnel or a baby bird is trying to fly for the first time—why, that ligament grows and pushes your claws out into the world. The word "phalanx," it may interest you to know, refers to a group of armed soldiers. Greeks in ships pulled by Abyssinian and Persian slaves destroyed each other in endless wars, and in each ship a phalanx waited for the signal to attack, and at the end of each soldier's leg his own little phalanx waited for the signal: to scratch, to claw, to shred. To kill without mercy. To rip flesh from bones and expose the tender throat to premolars, incisors, and canines. *What are you saying?* What I'm saying is that you and Buddy here have something in common. That's right: your favourite teeth are named after him: *canines*. They're part of you, as *he* is part of you. Let that sink in.

A murmur ran around the room. The judge lifted his gavel.

Oliver waited for his words to settle out into the truth he wanted—as with a trapped mouse, Carolyn thought. Daniel was becoming agitated: his good ear swivelled like an antenna as he looked around in apparent disbelief, then turned questioningly toward Carolyn. She shrugged.

—My friends, Oliver resumed, this dog's responsibility is self-evident. But remember: *only when necessary*. And what after all is necessary? Whatever is according to nature, fate, or chance. Did my client ask to be born a dog, to be tied to a laundry line in an overgrown yard with a broken gate and left alone to go slowly and inevitably mad? No. Was he asked by his sire and dame, whom he never knew, probably, whether he *wanted* to come into a world where his nature would earn him names like *monster*, *creature*, and *tiger*? If the ambiguity of the case makes confidence difficult, then I ask you to consider: what is necessary in your own nature? What alternative have *you* found to the conditions of your own birth? Oh, but we're all *good* cats, aren't we? Are you sure? Because until you understand what good Buddy *thought* would come of his actions you are not qualified to be his judges. And if you *can* judge, and judge impartially, rationally, and universally, you must perforce find him innocent. The necessity of your own—nay, *our* own— nature demands it. Let us, at least, who have laws and the power to choose, affirm the foundations of our dignity. For the sake of our children. Thank you.

Oliver turned swiftly and in one liquid motion leaped to the top of the filing cabinet and rested his chin on his forepaws.

There was a moment of stunned silence, then everyone began arguing with their neighbours; soon, shoving matches broke out in packed corners. The press gallery hoisted a wide-eyed Singapura back over the rail after she was elbowed from her seat by two boxing Korats, and the bailiff, a fearsome Lykoi with bright yellow eyes and coarse fur like a badger, walked back and forth batting the worst offenders until they sat down. Even the Burmese took off his hat and rubbed his thin pate as if he were trying to work out what he had heard. Then with an angry hiss he hurled his cigar blindly over his shoulder, barely missing Mr. Universe.

From amidst the commotion Daniel saw the judge rise and retreat through his curtain. A moment later he returned carrying something in his hand, and through the parted curtain Daniel spotted an opening—another door, perhaps a way out! He nudged Carolyn and nodded in the judge's direction.

—What?

—Maybe we'll get out alive after all. There's another door back there, I think.

—Or maybe you're being paranoid? I mean, what on earth did you *do*? Daniel? What?

He looked at her, and his eyes filled with shame and regret. She relented.

—*Vaillance* she said, placing her paw over his.

The gavel banged three times. The bailiff darted forward and fairly screeched: *Hear ye hear ye, this court is still in session!*

The crowd settled down instantly, as if in spontaneous mutual agreement to confirm whether any option but violence remained.

The Grey Nebelung spoke into the momentary calm. Buddy tugged, harder than before, but the chain held and only the jade eyes of the Maine Coon tracked him, coolly as ever.

—In all my years at the Citadel, the judge said, and I count myself among those few who in time almost beyond recall first walked these ruined halls and so named it—in all those years there has never been a case like this. There is nothing in the law, no guide in precept, precedent, or principle to help me—to help *us*, I may say, for I join you in being troubled at these events—identify a just solution. How do we solve the problem of a monster, whom we understand one is to address as "Buddy," when that ... person? ... that moral agency, let us say, is unambiguously a killer with the blood of our kinsmen on his torrid breath? *Is* he a person? Are we? Is *that* the question we face?

The judge shook his head, sighed, and withdrew from where he had concealed it under his robe a small leather bag that he placed on the bench. A hissing intake of breath whistled around the room. Two Torties who had been locked in fighting, one with his fangs in the fur of the other's neck, pushed each other off and stood back. The entire front row, apart from the mourners, took a step back.

—We are fortunate, dear friends, said the judge, that our wise forefathers and foremothers provided for moments such as these.

35

All of you know what this is, evidently, though few have perhaps seen it so close, and none recently. The last time was near the end of my predecessor's term of office; we cherish her memory. But the need has appeared again. Let it be clearly understood that I take no pleasure in this action. But the welfare of our civil polity—indeed, of our very community— depends upon our fidelity to the Founders in the shadow of whose wisdom we now stand. The marbles will decide: white, grey, and black. There is to be no appeal.

The Grey Nebelung untied the drawstring of the pouch and reached inside. The court held its breath. After a moment of rummaging he withdrew a closed paw. Turning it to the ceiling, he slowly unclenched his fist. A black marble lay nestled between his manicured claws.

The room exploded. The Torties immediately went back to each others' throats. Two Torbies linked paws and launched themselves at one of the grey-wigged magistrates, and all three fell to the floor in a writhing, screeching ball. The partition separating the litigants collapsed and a wave of enraged spectators spilled out and started fighting in the aisle. A Chausie in a dirty waistcoat choked a hapless Turkish Van next to him with the chain of his pocket-watch, while behind him a broad-shouldered Ragdoll in a leather vest climbed onto the splintered railing and projected herself horizontally at a pair of slender Munchkins hugging each other in fright. A beautiful Russian Blue scampered up the broken railing and jumped onto a vane of the ceiling fan; she arched her back and screamed at everyone in general, then batted out one of the candles with a paw.

At this Mr. Universe took notice. He left his post at the tunnel entrance and waded through the field of flying cats cuffing and thumping on both sides until he stood directly in front of the widows and widowers huddled in their row. There he resumed his guard, and anyone who strayed too close was sent tumbling.

Carolyn and Daniel had backed up against the wall when the commotion started and now flattened themselves and edged away from the tunnel entrance where the fighting was fiercest. Relying on stealth more than strength, they followed a path through the rioting cut by the enraged and blindly flailing Burmese, until a Pixiebob in blue overalls and a Ragamuffin with a pronounced underbite threw a coal sack over his head and dragged him out of sight. By then, however, they had almost circled the perimeter, and a few precise leaps brought them past the gallery, lawyers' boxes (Kitty and Oliver had disappeared at the first shriek), and clerk's desk. From behind the judge's bench they looked down on a sea of writhing and slashing with a sort of island in the middle of Mr. Universe swinging and pummeling like a machine.

—Good lord, said Carolyn. Daniel said nothing.

They reached the curtain behind the judge's bench. The judge had left, taking his marbles with him, and when Carolyn pulled back the heavy cloth a breath of cold air fluttered in her whiskers.

—OK, she said. You may have been right. Let's go.

She pulled Daniel through the curtain and then located, by smell more than sight in the dim antechamber, the source of the draft. She stumbled through a second curtain and suddenly they were standing in a narrow tunnel dimly lit by flickering candles mounted in haphazard sconces along one wall.

The floor sloped upward steeply, and after a short, hard climb the glowing outline of a door appeared at the end of the tunnel. A dusting lay on the floor where wind had driven snow through the cracks. Fortunately, the door was slightly ajar, and Carolyn and Daniel pushed together until it ground open onto deep snow. A bright landscape lay outside—too bright for their eyes after the tunnel—and they paused inside the threshold to catch their breath.

—There are no footprints, Daniel said, looking around at the floor. Wherever he went it wasn't here.

—Who cares? That was the most disgusting thing I've ever seen. That poor dog.

—That ... what? You're kidding! Did we see the same nightmare? The poor dog!

—Forget it. We have to figure out what to do. There's no going back. Not that way.

—OK. Survival. Well, what do we have to work with?

—Nothing.

—Right. Well, we could head home, wait till tomorrow and try again after the storm clears.

—We don't have a home anymore. Probably.

—Right. Well then maybe we should just wait. There's got to be food of some kind around here somewhere.

Carolyn stuck her head out the door and looked left and right. The wind had abated and snow was falling in large flakes through the yellow cone of a streetlight illuminating a concrete platform. The calm was disorienting after the pandemonium of the court, and when they stepped fully outside it took them a minute to become aware of a broad space receding into darkness and snow.

—It's beautiful, Carolyn said, or will be if we survive. Oh, those are train tracks. Look.

Four parallel ridges of undisturbed snow ran into darkness between high chainlink fences. The light, they realized, was not a streetlight at all but a utility light over a transformer in the middle of a rail yard.

—I think this is the Ossington, said Daniel, or part of it. It's a switching station. I was here once but summer and daytime. I'm not even sure which way is the lake. Let's just pick. It's fifty-fifty.

—Hm, said Carolyn The snow is almost over my head in places. If we keep under these bushes at the side over here. See? It's a little less.

There might be a break in the fence. We're not that far after all. There's a place I know where we could hole up for a while.

—We're not criminals.

—Did I say that?

—You said "hole up." We're not Bonnie and Clyde.

—Let's go.

Carolyn was growing increasingly unhappy, and not just because they were now in an even worse—in fact, a very *much* worse—spot than they had been. Something in Daniel's voice when he talked about the trial, about leaving their home behind—what, in the end, were they doing? In her mind she replayed their conversation before leaving, then recalled other leave-taking conversations from earlier in her life, before Daniel; a life not so very long as of yet, but already so different from the lives of other cats she had known. Cats like the smooth Abyssinian. Like Jack. Her steps wavered and clumps of snow from overhanging branches fell into her ears. She shook her head.

—Daniel, she said, why do you think that dog was guilty? You seemed convinced. I'm just asking.

Even amid crisis it pleased Daniel to be consulted.

—Oh, well, he said, I suppose the facts are plain enough. We spend half our lives running from dogs after all. What more is there to say?

—Yes, but what that defense lawyer said. Teeth and claws and all that. Oliver.

— We can retract our claws. A dog cannot. Violence is in their nature. It *is* their nature. We, on the other hand, have laws. Those laws allow us to choose.

—But if what is natural is good—because we're animals, too, right? so it has to be the same—if everyone is judged for what they are and every creature kills to eat, well who's to judge when the judge is a bag of marbles? What good is it to choose? That's what went wrong for Buddy, because otherwise it would be the same, right? That's what the lawyer meant. If only he'd said it plain so people could understand.

—It's all just lawyer talk. Sophistry. Socrates he is not.

—But is he *wrong*?

—There's nature and there's nature. We made the Five Laws. We built the Citadel.

—The Citadel inside the Ruin?

—So what? Don't be obtuse. Any dog deserves death a dozen times over. The conclusion is self-evident from first principles.

—Don't talk to me like one of your students. You're no better than anyone else you know despite your talk.

—Really. Who got us here?

—You did!

—Exactly! Anyhow, he said, glancing up at the sky. It's finally breaking up a little. I can see a clear patch.

Carolyn looked up. Yes. A few stars. A glimmer.

Daniel shrugged. There's nothing there either you know. Lights between clouds in a snowstorm that's slowing us down. Worse than useless: distracting. To survive in winter, keep moving. To survive in the world, think clearly. Right now we need to do both.

—The stars are beautiful though, even if they're empty, said Carolyn. Maybe especially.

They trudged on. Walking was less difficult under the bushes, as Carolyn had surmised, and the light of the power station faded into the gloom behind them; an identical gloom lay ahead. At first they kept their eyes on the spot where the tracks disappeared into darkness, but after a time it became easier just to hang their heads and watch each paw contend separately with its next step. Eventually, the weight of snow, the real weight known to those who have shifted it with their bodies, crept into their thoughts and numbed their limbs.

It occurred to Carolyn that they were going to die. They had long stopped talking, and in the silence her mind wandered drowsily among the words she would use when the end was certain. Her head drooped until her whiskers were just grazing the snow and her delicate pink nose became encrusted with ice. Glancing over her shoulder, she saw Daniel plodding behind her, no longer even bothering to follow in her steps. The tenebrous outline of his body wavered as if they were both already ghosts.

It was long past midnight when, creeping wearily around a thick cluster of overhanging branches, Carolyn stumbled over a soft obstruction half-buried in the snow. She was in such a torpor of exhaustion and despair that she fell to her knees right up against whatever it was. Instinctively, she pawed at the snow to see if the thing could be moved.

She let out a gasp. Emerging from the snow between her paws, the outline of a small golden-brown dog lay curled as if asleep. A tattered bindle lay nearby.

—Daniel! Carolyn called. Daniel came up to her and looked down. They exchanged a glance.

— What? How? Where?

—Help me.

—Help you what? It's a dog!

— It's a dog the size of a hamster. And I think it's still alive. Look!

The dog had wrapped its tiny paws around its nose to fend off the cold, but a little vaporous mist showed between the protruding fangs of its underbite. Carolyn cleared more snow from the flat face and bent to listen. The dog's breathing was shallow and ragged. Daniel peered over her shoulder.

—I've seen one of those before, at the zoo. Walking in the zoo I mean. *Griffon Bruxellois*. A ratter. Belgian.

—He's half rat himself. Help me get him out of the ice. He's stuck.

41

They pulled and scraped with their claws, and for an instant the dog's eyes slitted open without comprehension. They freed the back paws and nearly hairless belly and extricated the lumpy form to the top layer of snow. But they were too weak themselves to carry him far, and, besides, there was nowhere to go. An impassable embankment lay on one side and thick, snow-laden bushes on the other, and steel fences beyond on either side. Forward and back were unchanged. Daniel shifted side to side and Carolyn suddenly realized she couldn't feel her own feet. How had this ridiculous creature survived? Where was he going? Where had he come from? How did he end up on railway tracks in a snowstorm?

—Daniel, Carolyn said. We can't just leave.

— No, of course not. Why not?

Carolyn regarded Daniel critically. Half his face was caked in snow from walking with his missing ear turned opposite the wind. His tail dragged. One eye was nearly closed. She wondered how she looked to him and took momentary comfort in her missing tail. But she could barely stand up, and her vision swam with black specks and wispy curls of light; between them they were barely one cat, neither alive nor dead. Hopelessness and the absurdity of their predicament crowded upon her. Why hadn't a train cleared a path? Had they stopped running? She looked at Daniel again, then at the sleeping dog. Something in the dog's crumpled helplessness awoke inside her. She made a decision.

She turned to face Daniel.

—You never really understood why I paint. My art. You never really got it. You supported me and I'm grateful for that but you never understood.

—What?

—It has to cost you everything, Daniel. A painting is anything you want it to be but only next to everything it might have been that was left out. You have to see it all. You at least have to try. That's what art is. That's what love is, too. You have to trust both sides. You never understood. I didn't understand myself until now. And I don't think you ever will.

Daniel looked into the identical featureless landscape ahead and behind, the buried tracks, the leaden sky. He looked at the still form of the dog lying in the snow, then at Carolyn.

—You're just saying this because we don't have kids.

—Goats have kids. I'm talking about happiness.

—Listen, Carolyn. We have to keep moving. Do you understand? *We are going to die.*

—Yes. That's why I'm staying. Go on if you want. It's probably not much farther. The snow is starting to let up.

Daniel stared in astonishment and confusion, then held out an encrusted paw.

—I love you.

She didn't answer except to sit down with her back legs tucked around the dog and her head bowed to keep off the falling snow. Daniel squinted at the tracks ahead as though measuring the distance; then he closed his eyes and tried to feel the entire universe under his feet, in his fur, in his whiskers, in his lungs, on his face, in the hollow of his one ear. Then, sitting opposite Carolyn, he tucked his hind legs identically around the dog's other side and leaned toward her until their foreheads met. And there they sat pooling their heat, two cats in love with the world.

A is for Angel

Angels departed long ago. Nevertheless, I overheard this one night in a playground.

There is the ordinary world where everything is as it seems: rakes and rocks, chickens and churches, paperweights and paper. In

43

the world below that you are lying in bed too worried for sleep and everything is something else. That world both is and is not a subterranean river inhabited by either blind or sighted fish who may or may not have razor teeth. Below that the archangels of true ideas sing without taking a breath and glide on feathery wings that brush you sometimes like a stray touch from a lover. Below that is only primordial fire that hovers just above the ordinary world and illuminates its edges for those who can see: rakes and rocks, chickens and churches, paperweights and paper.

A is for Anghared

I had a raven once named Anghared. She was a pet, a gift from an eccentric aunt. The name was a secret known only to the raven and me; everyone else called her "Ann Herod" and wondered why a raven was named for a biblical tyrant. I never wrote her name anywhere, not even on her gravestone in our garden. It was a plain stone that only I knew was a gravestone. Anghared was a Welsh princess and warrior. Her name means *one who is beloved*.

A is for Anticipation

Everyone has heard of Pavlov's drooling dogs. The story is so well known that I can say "Pavlov's drooling dogs" and you know what's coming; you hear the bell. But not everyone knows Pavlov used to shock his German Shepherds, too; it wasn't all treats. Pavlov was pleased but not surprised when he rang the bell and the Shepherds, loyal in their cages, their trusting intelligent eyes, trembled both for the bell and for the discovery that the world could contain so much inexplicable cruelty and pain. Pleased, Pavlov noted in his journal, but not surprised.

A is for Antihypertriton

The Ridgeview had neither ridge nor view but did have velvety orange wallpaper and a carpet pockmarked as an overcooked pancake. It also had good high windows that on clear afternoons reflected sunlight from windshields in the parking lot and illuminated the wood paneling back to the sticky booths. The windows were continuous along the front of the shops and restaurants until an overhang divided the plaza at right angles; a dusty and litter-strewn alley lay between. Kids from the high school across the street would stand under the overhang in circles and smoke and talk and kick the ambient trash and look down the alley to the back of the plaza for the empty pallets and plastic milk crates stacked there sometimes. On windy afternoons miniature cyclones of grit and dry leaves whipped down the alley until the kids saw in each others' faces the absolute knowledge of cigarette butts swollen open in the rain like turned-out bullets. At such moments you could stand ten feet from the frozen yoghurt place and it was far enough to mock the rich kids going for a Raspberry Explosion at lunch. Ten feet and miles off.

Glancing out the window periodically Daniel nursed a lukewarm cup of black coffee and ignored the doughnut that maintained him as a paying customer: *I'm eating. Leave me alone.* A book lay open on the table with its thin edge pinned under a plate.

He was waiting for someone and also he was not. Her material appearance was distinctly unlikely. He had instead decided to wait for the idea of her to become clear in his mind. This happened easily when he looked outside: her silhouette wended through dazzling windshields toward the door of the restaurant. Then he returned to his book and after a few distracted paragraphs looked again. An hour of this had left his donut stale and reduced his sips of coffee to discrete inhalations.

The door opened and a man stepped into the airlock between the restaurant's inner and outer doors. Daniel was mildly surprised. He hadn't seen anyone cross the parking lot except kids going to the variety store on the opposite corner.

The man looked around and sat down at a table near Daniel. The server gave him a menu and he ran his finger down the plastic page like he was speed reading. Pancakes. Double order. Extra syrup. Sweet tooth eh? Gotcha.

Could have sat anywhere. Pancakes?
—Hello there.

Daniel swiveled his eyes from the page without moving his head.

The man was above forty. Bigger than he looked with a salt and pepper crew-cut and stained greenish coat in indeterminate style. He looked at Daniel with a mildly genial expression and Daniel noted his almost transparent eyelashes.

—Hello Daniel said and shifted the doughnut closer to the book side of the plate.

The man took off his coat and draped it over the back of his chair.

—If I may take the entirely gratuitous liberty of an observation: you look like someone waiting for someone.

—Just enjoying my lunch Daniel said. And reading. He showed open pages to the man and laid the book carefully back down on its cover. *Never talk to strangers.*

—So I see. Well I won't intrude. The man swept crumbs off the table and looked around. He did this not casually but cranking back and forth in his chair and leaning over to peer into booths and behind the nearly empty dessert counter.

—It's not much to look at said Daniel.

—So I. Yes. It's alright. I've seen worse I daresay. The man's accent seemed an even blend of the world and oddly musical. *Daresay*.

—Are you looking for someone? I know most of the regulars here. Daytime regulars at least. And you look like someone looking for someone. If I may take the liberty.

He intended this as a parting shot but the man only smiled more broadly. Daniel looked out the window again and the stranger's eyes flicked over his profile.

—How are the pancakes?

—What?

—The pancakes. He gestured toward the empty table. I just ordered.

—I didn't get the pancakes. I don't get pancakes. See? He tilted up his plate and doughnut.

—Ah but you said you know the daytime regulars. So you're here often enough or perhaps assuming a random distribution of customers close enough to breakfast that you must have tried the pancakes yourself at some point or at least know someone who has. A reasonable inference no?

—They're just pancakes.

—So I should expect nothing out of the ordinary?

—Look around and take a guess what you can expect.

—Well said. Well said indeed. But one never can tell.

—Sometimes one can.

—Could you tell I would say "you look like someone waiting for someone?"

—I suppose not.

—And you said I looked like a man looking for someone. I didn't expect that either.

—Life is full of mysteries.

—So it is. And every stage its own: Need. Curiosity. Freedom. Responsibility. Holding on. Letting go. It gives one pause does it not? What are you reading by the way?

The stranger had leaned forward.

Daniel concealed his irritation for the faint hope of all readers to lead someone new into the charmed circle. He held up the cover.

—*The Black Cloud*. Fred Hoyle. It's a novel. Science fiction.

—Hoyle! So it is. Everything Hoyle wrote was science fiction. Good head for radar though. Worked countermeasures during the war. World War Two I mean.

—Huh. Most people think he invented playing cards. What do you have against him?

—Because I said he wrote science fiction? Nothing. And of course one cannot fault him for his era. Really I shouldn't be so quick to judge. There's more than enough mystery in the world for something new every now and then even if it's dead wrong. Don't you think?

Daniel considered.

—The steady-state. You're talking about steady-state theory. Before the Big Bang. Huh.

—Am I? Hoyle invented the phrase 'Big Bang' I believe did he not? And yet he hated the idea. Funny no?

—No. You've read him.

—Obviously. But not deeply no. In fact I might just have heard of him. Now that I think of it I'm not sure I've read him at all. Maybe it was when I was your age and I forgot. What a thing eh? The age you are now I hardly remember. Maybe you won't remember yourself when you're my age. That odd novel you read once. Once upon a time in a diner with unremarkable pancakes. He laughed. You know I fell out of a tree once when I was a kid. My brother dared me. The branch was rotten and I went out too far. I've always wondered whether he knew. The branch split and I tumbled down and landed on my side on the lawn and cracked three ribs. Took me months to recover. Had to sneeze with a pillow packed around me for the pain. The funny thing is sometimes I have to really think to remember which side it was on. Imagine that. He laughed again. The things that bother you now eh? Keep you up at night? Maybe you won't remember either. Maybe you will. Who knows? It takes courage to be young. When you walk a knife edge the straight line cuts your feet they say. So you have my sympathy. Does that matter? Does it matter to you personally or shall we say in the abstract? Does it matter in Hoyle's universe if a stranger says "you have my sympathy"? or perhaps "I'd like to help you if I can"?

Daniel tore off a corner of his napkin inserted it between the pages of his book and closed it with a soft thump. He took a bite of his doughnut.

—Well he said. Here's the thing. I don't know you and I'm here at the Ridge having lunch this pleasant afternoon. Maybe it's going to rain tonight but it's. Well I'd just call it a pleasant afternoon after an unseasonably hot and dry summer. And my coffee's gone cold and I think I'm at the unwelcome end of my so-called bottomless refills. So on the whole it seems unlikely yours or anybody's hypothetical conjectured or putative sympathy or lack thereof will amount to much at this juncture. No offense.

Daniel exercised his vocabulary for these occasions the way some men lifted weights. It was all the *thank you no* a reasonable person should need. But the stranger only lifted his eyebrows.

—Of course. Then again why not? What's the difference between here and now and any other shall we say occasion for sympathy? There's a Neolithic warmth in your blood that betrays you. And maybe you know just maybe—ah.

The pancakes had arrived.

The stranger poured a golden ring of maple syrup and attacked the pile with only a fork. He sawed and speared mouth-sized stacks with surprising vigor. When the pancakes were gone he poured a thinner ring of syrup around the edge of his plate and swirled loose crumbs into a golden slurry. When that was gone as well he licked the plate clean without any outward self-consciousness.

—Sometimes he said and laid the plate carefully back down on the table the problem is just not enough pancakes. Too little too late as they say.

—What's that?

—Pancakes.

—Hard to come by where you're from?

The man chuckled and hitched his chair around to face Daniel.

—My name's Fisher he said. Charles. Actually Hilbert Charles. But would you call yourself Hilbert if there was a viable alternative? No you would not. So. Most people call me Charlie. Or Chuck. With apologies to my parents.

—Daniel. No one calls me Dan. Or Danny.

—Nice to meet you Daniel.

—Same.

The man hitched his chair still closer and Daniel noticed a pale scar starting under his right ear and running below his collar.

—Sorry to interrupt. Are you—?

—No it's fine. It's not much of a lunch. I didn't actually mean to be rude just now by the way. It's just that I'm.

—You're reading. Of course. Who am I? Nobody. A stranger in a restaurant. No need to apologize. None at all.

—OK.

—OK.

The man crossed his fork and unused knife on the plate and wiped his hands on his jacket and pants. He looked at Daniel appraisingly.

—I tell you what Daniel. May I tell you a story? *That's odd he said. A story? How peculiar!* It isn't much. But I presented myself just now as a person of what shall we call it? "You have my sympathy" I said and "I'd like to help you." Well there's no sympathy like a story if you believe it. Then you'll learn something about me too and we can become friends. "Life is full of mysteries" you said. And I have just a little while and you want to get back to your book. What do you say? Let me just order some coffee first.

He ordered two coffees. Daniel fidgeted with his plate and cup. Looked outside. It was past noon. The sun was just tipping west.

—I can buy my own coffee.

—Of course you can. But permit me. So formal—"permit me." But no one bought me coffee when I was your age. Not that I would necessarily remember as we were discussing. But as I search my memory I cannot recall a single instance in my youth in which I was purchased coffee. So. Permit me.

—Well I won't argue.

The coffee arrived and Daniel added twice his usual amount of sugar and stirred twice as long. Hilbert Charles Fisher busied himself with a notebook extracted from one of his coat's many pockets. He flipped pages back and forth.

—Is this uh story in your notes? I thought you meant a joke or something.

—No no. Yes though in a way. A joke. Yes. I just need. OK.

He flapped the book closed and returned it to his jacket. Tested his coffee. Added more sugar. Stirred the coffee with the blade of his knife.

—We were talking about World War Two just now. Where I'm from there was a place. A school. Actually it was an animal hospital and later it became a school. Once upon a time there were sick animals getting better in pens and then children learning math in classrooms and hanging up coats in cloakrooms. A row of muddy boots in the hall. Umbrellas hanging on hooks. Imagine being those

51

walls eh? Animals first then children. What a world you'd say. *What happened? I have no idea.* It was after the war. World War One I mean. Do you follow so far?

—You have no idea how to tell a story do you?

—It's not my specialty. I'm an engineer. Of sorts.

—Well keep going. Once upon a time there was an animal hospital.

—And a school. In that order. That'll become important later.

—Why not just tell me now why it's important?

—Because you have to understand *why* it's important.

—That's what I'm saying: tell me straight off so I know what to look for.

—I *am* telling you straight off!

—OK. Keep going.

—So there was an animal hospital in the south of England. That's plain enough. I can say "once upon a time there was an animal hospital in the south of England" and you get a picture right away. Horses. Targhees. Bluefaced Leicester. A clean house with windows and a brick chimney overgrown with ivy like something out of James Herriot. The smiling vet at the door in a white coat. But that's already wrong. But will you listen otherwise? So. There was an animal hospital near Stonehenge in the south of England during World War One. Most of the able-bodied men were off fighting in France and Belgium and there wasn't much in the way of medical supplies. Not for domestic animals at least. It wasn't a good time to be a Jacob or a Badger-face Welsh Mountain. Sick or injured animals were simply killed. Euthanized we would say now. I should mention incidentally that this animal hospital didn't exist yet. Yes there was a hospital on Salisbury Plain and yes it was founded by a young woman named Amelia that you haven't met yet. But right now she exists and the hospital doesn't. You follow?

—You haven't actually said anything but sure.

— So. Amelia. Her father was killed in Gallipoli a year before.

— A year before what?

—A year before she left for the animal hospital.

—Why did she leave?

—Who's telling the story?

—My apologies. Please continue.

—Amelia lived on a farm in Hampshire with her mother and four sisters and brothers. Her mother took a train to Southampton twice a week for shifts she shared with two other widows who were struggling. This means struggling for food you understand. It's the dead of winter 1917. At the factory where she works the mother hears about a farmer who's donated land for use as a shelter of some sort for sick animals. The idea is to turn the shelter into a kind of field hospital with support from local government and so on. Because there's a need you see. So this becomes the animal hospital. Right now it's just a field though. Actually it's a field again. Anyhow the mother knows Amelia is good with animals because of the farm and helping neighbours and so forth. The mother also knows one less mouth to feed is one less mouth to feed. So arrangements are made. A friend knows the farmer. A ticket is purchased. Soon enough Amelia finds herself on a steam train to Southampton. Then she walks to Salisbury. *Walks.* She's 17. You have no idea. What can I do but repeat it slowly? She took a train to Southampton. Then she walked to Salisbury. So. In Russia food's getting scarce and Lenin is trying to convince farmers that the true enemy is the Romanovs and not the Kaiser. *What does that have to do with anything?* You have to listen.

So Amelia's mother sends her to Southampton to Salisbury and she starts working at the shelter-hospital. It's hard because the work is hard obviously but also she's far from home and it's 1917 and she's a young woman with a job in rural England in wartime. You follow?

—I follow. Walking all the way.

—Excellent. So the farmer checks in every now and then and it's fine. The hospital starts making money and eventually a barn rises over the tent. It's early 1918. The American Expeditionary Force lands in France. Amelia is a natural they say and before you know it she's practically running the place. You have no idea what I'm saying. When farmers' Dorset Downs go down they take them to a now 18-year-old Amelia who's self-taught and running a successful animal hospital in a field near Stonehenge in 1918. It's extraordinary.

—If you say so.

—Then the war ends and everyone goes home. Hurrah. But for Amelia it's the end. The need evaporates. Now there's a baby boom. And because she's very clever Amelia realizes that what's needed is a school. Babies are popping up like Speckle-face Beulahs. Those are kinds of sheep by the way. They're all kinds of sheep. I've made what you would call a private study. What I'm saying is "animals were out and babies were in."

—I get it. Is this going somewhere?

—So Amelia talks to the farmer and asks if it's alright to turn the hospital into a small independent school. Well the farmer's wife caught a fever over the winter and died and he's gone funny as a result. He says children will upset his cows etcetera. Also he lost his brother in the war—literally lost. The body was never found. And somehow the missing brother got mixed up in the farmer's head with the children and he starts wandering the countryside trying to find one or the other. That's not the story though. I think children kept the grief fresh in his mind but I don't know. I'm not a psychologist. I had an uncle once who used to sneak cigars but stopped smoking after his wife died because he said she hated the smell. I have no idea. Anyway he was opposed to the school and fought Amelia on it. Then he died. He caught the fever same as his wife and kicked the same milking pail. So it goes. But on his deathbed he signed over the property in perpetuity to Amelia. Why? A midnight visit from the ghostly eidolon of John Dewey? It's impossible to say. The salient point is Amelia is free and clear to run her school. It's August 1919. The Weimar Republic is born. By autumn she's heavily in debt and taking on her first students. Why does that matter you ask? Do you want more coffee? OK.

So the students start to arrive. Most are dirt poor or orphans or both. And two of the first—now pay attention—are the twins Alva and Aidan Perrin. They arrive from Derry via parents untroubled by the prospect of an English education. Now these twins were mathematical geniuses but not yet. The oak was still in the acorn as they say. Though I've never understood the expression. Everything an oak will ever do is in the acorn but an oak doesn't mature until it's 30 years old. If you talked to a 25-year-old oak tree and told it about acorns it would have no idea what you were talking about: *what the hell are acorns you stupid old man? Fake news!* Then five years later it's loaded with acorns. Where was the plan in the meantime? Now you be the tree and I'll be the man: *now then my good fellow what unexpressed acorns of good or evil might lie in store for the human race in five years hmm? Why what acorns might even be slumbering in you my young friend?* There's a moral for you to make it a proper story: always believe in yourself. And check your acorns.

Daniel suppressed a savage retort and reflexively looked out the window for oaks. He found Manitoba maples in raised square boxes clinging to life in the parking lot. His companion looked at him thoughtfully as if waiting for a response. Daniel started pulling his cardboard coaster apart like warm taffy.

—Well. I can perhaps guess what you're thinking. Every young man wants to believe in a world that wants what he has and has what he wants. I understand. You have my sympathy as I have said. Of course I have the advantage of remembering my defeats instead of anticipating them. Most of them. He shrugged. A man my age just wants to believe the music he listened to in his first car can still change the world. Do you like The Beatles?

—Not specifically. Do you like Popol Vuh?

—Who?

—I guess there's still hope for one of us.

—Indeed. To continue. Amelia taught the twins as best she could and gave them a good start. Then they were accepted at a regional middle school and from there a very good private school on scholarship after they jointly solved Landau's Prime Conjecture in a national contest at the age of 16. That's a math puzzle. Are you an aficionado? You are not. Amid growing fame they attend none other than the University of Copenhagen and the Institute for Theoretical Physics under the great Niels Bohr himself. They attend the Fifth Solvay Conference in 1927. They're even in the famous picture but got stuck behind Auguste Piccard. Only Pauli seemed to notice. Now it's 1929. Gustav Stresemann has just died. Germany pledges international peace in return for lower war reparation payments to salvage its imploding economy. The world stands at a crossroads.

In Copenhagen the twins shoot up the academic ranks. After a stunning series of mathematical proofs and discoveries in the foundations of quantum physics they become international celebrities. They lunch with Einstein in Paris. Herbert Hoover welcomes them to New York City. Awards and accolades pile up. They're given a staff of researchers and experimentalists and start working with George Gamow on quantum tunneling and particle decay and the still dimly-lit mysteries of the atomic nucleus.

—Gamow. Another Big Bang guy. I've read about him.

—Does that seem like a coincidence?

—I don't understand.

—Hm. So the twins begin working with Gamow on the mysteries of space and time. All three are young and ambitious and in their productive prime for physicists which is generally young. They're about the same age you are now.

Before long however they start to disagree with Bohr privately and then in public. They're convinced the Copenhagen Interpretation of the so-called collapse of the wave function is incomplete in ways Bohr refuses to consider. Bohr's hypnotized by the math they say but the twins have something bigger in mind. In 1932 they leave Copenhagen to work on the new cyclotron at the Radium Institute in Leningrad. You've heard of it? Of course not. Why would you? Hindenburg is still alive. German diplomats are in Geneva arguing against limits on military expansion under the Treaty of Versailles. Amelia Earhart is in the air over Ireland in her trusty Lockheed Electra. Goofy is born. Babe Ruth hits a home run.

In Leningrad the twins turn the physics world upside down. Within a year they map or predict most of the elementary particles. They quantify the electron. The lambda baryon. They discover the K meson and assorted hyperons. The hypertriton. And then. In a flash of shared genius unparalleled in the history of scientific thought they predict the charge mass and spin of the antihypertriton and devise a method to stabilize it between counter-rotating magnetic monopoles in a vessel of sintered beryllium oxide. After that, everything changes.

The antihypertriton has an energy density greater than any substance known, indeed greater than any possible. In precise configurations it can bend space on minute scales and even, some misguided heretics in the faculty lounge dared whisper, even create the preconditions to reverse entropy.

In brief, the antihypertriton remade the world. Safe, clean, and relatively cheap energy from a virtually inexhaustible source. After the initial paper, the twins published the design of the containment and utilization system, none other than the great helix coils themselves, without patent or encumbrance, and soon power plants start popping up all over the world. That was the beginning. By the end of the decade most of the world's production of coal, oil, and natural gas is winding down. A thousand catastrophes are averted. The Weimar Republic is replaced by the Democratic Republic of Germany, and Berlin becomes the hub of a peaceful coalition extending from Leningrad to Washington. The League of Nations moves its headquarters to Kaliningrad and initiates the Seven Bridges Project, which for three decades spurs international development and cooperation on an unprecedented scale. Freed from endless proxy wars and the burden of empire, the Soviet Union sheds its satellite states and becomes a loose federation. NATO and the Warsaw Pact are never born. Eventually, the League of Nations itself is retired in all but name. The twenty-first century dawns on an era of peace and prosperity.

Despite their fame, the twins never forgot their beginning. There was a picture on the cover of *Life* where Alva and Aidan are shaking hands with Amelia in front of a construction site. They're laughing. Amelia looks older. I kept that picture until it fell apart. I don't know what the building was—probably school improvements they were funding and so on. The twins endowed a library in Baltimore and named it after Amelia, and March 24, the date they arrived at the school, was proclaimed the Day of International Amity and celebrated across the globe.

So then. *What's the point?* you ask. The point is that Amelia became the indirect savior of humankind because of choices that aligned particular causes with particular effects at crucial times. Those choices radically altered the human future, and even the animal future: that building saved more animals as a school than as a hospital. So it goes that way, too, sometimes, I suppose. Anyhow, nothing would have happened without that first step. If she hadn't walked to Salisbury to build an animal hospital at the heart of Stonehenge we might not be having this conversation right now. We might not be here at all, you understand? So. I guess that's the end. You're welcome.

Daniel looked at him with a sneer of mingled disgust and disbelief. He shoved his plate away as if it were culpable.

—As you would say, he said, *what the hell was that? he said.* I mean, I wasn't expecting Robert McKee, but you have to admit.

—Why?

Daniel stared at his doughnut. The icing he'd been saving for his fingers had soaked into the collapsing dough and left an unappetizing mucilaginous paste. Charles Fisher shifted subtly in his seat until they seemed to face each other across a long table. Daniel arranged his cup, book, plate, spoon, and coaster fragments into rough symmetry.

—OK. Let's just take it for what it is, because why not. Just for fun shall we say. Even so, that story was complete idiotic rambling nonsense.

—Really? Why?

—Start with the logic. This Amelia, you say, is the indirect savior of humankind. A library in Baltimore. March is the international day of etcetera. Based on choices and effects. OK. But why does she get the credit? If you wanted a moral about decisiveness, there are better candidates. Why not the farmer who donated the land? Or the wife who died—or, for that matter, the virus that killed her? That had a role. It played a part. Or how about Kaiser Wilhelm, or the Black Hand who triggered the war that created the need for a hospital in the first place? Or the soldier brother who disappeared and paved the way for the farmer's otherwise inexplicable but highly convenient deathbed conversion? I concede the twins' credit for the hypothetical hypermegatron—sure, why not. But the poor Irish parents—why not give *them* the Nobel Prize, if only for hack stereotypes? Oh, I'm assuming the twins won the Nobel at some point.

—They did. Twice. Once for physics and once for peace, in that order. Alva donated her portion to the SPCA.

Daniel rolled his eyes.

— Listen, though, Daniel. May I call you Dan? I cannot. Take out Amelia and the picture disappears. *That's the point.* What are the odds otherwise? Doubt all you want, but facts are facts.

—Facts, sure, not random hallucinations with animals. A chance thing happening doesn't make an equally chance thing less likely just because it didn't happen. Throw a deck of cards off a building and you'll get some poker hands: three of a kind, maybe a full house. So what? *Something* has to turn up, and you don't get to choose beforehand except in stories, obviously!

— No need to shout! And I agree, wholeheartedly. But only one set of hands turns up, you know, to use your example. It's either hearts or clubs, two pair or four aces.

—Alright. Let me try again. Have you ever seen the Bayeux Tapestry? The Battle of Hastings? Edward the Confessor, the childless king and his contested throne? You know how many times Harold and William appear in panel after panel? It's over a hundred feet long! So which is the true Harold and William? The Harold landing in Normandy? The one standing under Halley's Comet? The one shot dead through the eye by an arrow at the end?

—Indeed. One might say that's precisely why there's a tapestry at all. QED. Oh, *quod erat demonstrandum* is Latin for "it has been shown."

—I know that! But the cards are rigged, is my point. What are the odds you'd walk in this morning while I'm reading Hoyle, and maybe you've read him, too—*maybe.* Then we wind up having this particular inane slash random conversation? *What are the odds?* you'd say. *A miracle!*

—Maybe I would.

—Don't try to be mysterious. I used to do it for a living.

Untroubled to conceal it, Daniel looked out the window for a focus to his irritation. A column of yellow buses caterpillared slowly around the corner toward the high school. Preparing for a summary departure, he flipped *The Black Cloud* around to put its spine in his palm and inadvertently clattered against his cup and saucer. He glared at his doughnut, then returned to the window and bit his lip.

It could be anything. Even now. And now. And now.

His companion regarded him coolly, then tapped a finger on the arm of his chair.

—You know what we need? he said. For a little clarity? Smoke! Do you smoke? You smoke. He checked the tables around him. Not here though.

Daniel tilted up his coffee cup and looked.

—I know a place, he said.

Hilbert Charles Fisher stood smoking under the overhang. A wind from the south, straightened by the plaza windows, sent knee-high whirlwinds of dry leaves, dust, wrappers, cigarette butts, and the chewed-off plastic tips of wine-dipped cigarillos down the alley toward him. Daniel, a pace behind, picked a spot nearer the wall and flipped his hair out of his eyes to light a cigarette from his Zippo. But his plan to luxuriate in blue plumes was carried away on the wind, so to punish the wind he hooked a finger over the perforated filter on his cigarette and inhaled until the nicotine seared his lungs and ballooned in his brain. A sudden stronger gust made both men pull their chins into their jacket-collars against the flying grit.

—It's been dry, Daniel said as if in general apology. Even April was dry as a rat. What can you do? Climate change we're supposed to call it now.

—Too bad the world turned out this way, eh? If only someone had made a different choice at a precise moment.

Daniel shook his head and scuffed at a stray cigarette butt and mangled wrapper from a Blueberry Burst. Through deft coordination of his left heel and right toe he managed to flick the butt into the wrapper in one attempt. To celebrate, he considered making some excuse to his companion and simply walking away across the parking lot. The excuse would need only a moment's plausibility. After all, who was Chuck Fisher to him? On the other hand, who was anyone to anyone? He shook his head again and scuffed.

—OK, he said after a minute. Since you're so inquisitive, and since I don't actually care, I'll tell you: I'm waiting for my ex. I told her I'd be here and maybe we could get together and talk and so on and so forth. We used to have lunch here when she worked at an art gallery downtown. *The Atelier*. Well you know how it goes.

His companion laughed. Do I? Maybe I've forgotten.

—We were engaged. At least I think we were. I guess that was part of the problem. We didn't talk about it but we seemed to be going in that direction. It was, shall we say, in the cards. Then something happened.

—Happened?

—I don't know. We got kicked out of our apartment. She didn't want to go and we argued about it. You have to be in the picture she said, and I wasn't, whatever that means. So we broke up. The end. Directed by Alan Smithee.

The stranger nodded and exhaled an enormous blue cloud into a moment of comparative calm. He looked around at the littered and dusty pavement with an expression of resignation tinged with recognition, and his words when he spoke seemed addressed to himself.

—The essence of manhood is self-sacrifice, he said tonelessly, and looked at Daniel.

Daniel stared at him in disbelief.

—*Manhood?* Really? Pray, what is the essence of womanhood?

—Self-sacrifice.

—I see. Well that's just grim.

—Maybe it is and maybe it isn't. Maybe beauty is a way for sympathy to come into the world. Maybe that's how we endure time. Maybe that's what art really is, and maybe love, too: sympathy in time.

He looked at Daniel with something like hope.

—Groovy, man. Anyway, I gotta go. It was nice meeting you, I guess. So long.

He flicked his cigarette away and pitched the empty pack into the alley, where it settled among the leaves and dust.

A is for Apsis

I first heard the word *apsis* in church one night when I was 12 and decided to learn it through and through. We didn't go to church very often, only when I was very young and we had moved again and for a while my parents would want to feel like part of a community. That would last about a month.

It was either Christmas or Easter. The minister met us at the door and greeted us easily and cheerfully, as though we were coming over for dinner. During the sermon he talked about the trinity and every now and then glanced over his shoulder to the high hollow end of the church and a table draped in white cloth, and behind that a stained glass hexagon, and over that an enormous, tapering wooden cross, and high over all a white dome painted in gold and blue stars with a billowing heaven and inscriptions in Latin that overflowed onto the wooden beams of the vaulted ceiling.

I was bored. I knew the sermon would be very long and that at some point the minister would take out a tissue to wipe away sweat from his face, and that when he did this bits of tissue would adhere to the bristle on his upper lip. I dreaded this moment.

White tapers had been distributed down the pews when we sat down, and I awaited the moment when the sermon ended and the minister carried the large Paschal candle solemnly from altar to front pew and the holy fire was passed taper to taper and lit up each worshipping face in turn. I awaited the moment because behind my back I had secretly crumbled the top half of my taper, concealing the paraffin wax fragments behind me on the pew. My sister saw what I was doing and covered her mouth with suppressed glee. Then, when the tapers were all alight, including my own wicked torch, the minister turned to the front of the church with its high dome glowing over the congregation and said *here in the apsis of our church in the presence of God let us pray* and bowed his head. Throughout the church there was silence. And it seemed to me that all the candles were burning as one, even my delinquent bonfire, and that the flame was like God singing, and the glow from the dome was God's joy shining from on high, so that my skull reverberated with shimmering silence like the apsis, the dome of the church: a burning bone hollow filled with glory.

A is for Arbitrary

When you die, depending on the exact circumstances, you wake up in a new universe where chance has taken one or another turn. The difference could be anything. Maybe the sky is white and the sun is blue or you're an inch taller or shorter. Maybe there are heroic dolphins who become successful test pilots despite a family history of dipsomania exploring new continents in squishy airsuits designed by dolphin NASA, who plant flags of dolphin conquest on the shores of dolphin New Mexico. Maybe you're a poet, or an architect, or a connoisseur of aardvark vocalizations who travels the breadth of Africa recording clips for your esoteric mixed-media sound collages. Maybe you're a girl or a boy or neither or both. Maybe your alphabet starts with the letter Z. Maybe you're not even human. But whatever you are, you are joined to this universe with a degree of freedom to intervene in its affairs. Even if you're only a clump of grass or a sunset or a seabird, you're the one people pray to when they're alone and afraid, even if they don't know who you really are or how to talk to you. This is why miracles are so rare.

A is for Aroma

Nora opened her eyes and took in the bed, embroidered pillow covers, half-open window, sunshine, ceiling, and walls. Then, as every morning, she shouldered the unseen until it returned her to her life. And Bailey, who was never wrong, leaped onto the pillow beside her and licked her face before jumping to the floor and trotting toward the kitchen in search of breakfast.

Nora put on the housecoat she had thrown onto a chair the previous evening and slid her feet into the laceless sneakers Daniel used for slippers and shuffled after Bailey. At the top of the stairs, the aroma of frying eggs and the morning sounds of her family drifted around her like an embrace.

Daniel was at the stove. He glanced at Bailey and smiled at Nora.

—Morning. Nice shoes. Did you see Bailey dreaming again? I love watching him dream. Did you know dogs dream whatever it is they are? I read about it in *The Guardian*, I think, a long time ago. Some scientists cut out the part of the dog's brain that keeps them from moving in their sleep, then filmed them sleeping. It turns out dogs dream whatever they do in real life: pointers point, retrievers retrieve, shepherds herd, just as though they're awake. Old and decrepit as he is I think Bailey still chases rabbits and squirrels every night. I'd love to do that.

—Yes, you *have* told me. Is there any coffee?

Daniel filled a mug from the percolator on the stove and handed it to her.

—Fresh.

Nora inhaled deeply through her nose over the steaming mug.

—I don't know what we ever had against chicory. Could use some milk though. Where's Azalea?

—Still in bed. It's only 10.

They laughed.

—I'll pick up some more milk this afternoon, Daniel said. I think we can afford it. Another litre's tricky when it's three of us and already Wednesday. Just give me a second to finish these eggs. There's toast, too, if you want.

Nora sipped. From the second bedroom upstairs came a thud.

—Eggs won't hold her.

Daniel popped in two more slices and set a plate in front of Nora.

—I heard some good news. Jeff Tanner says there'll be power all the way around the pond in a couple of weeks if they can get the poles in and the weather holds. They need someone who can hook up a step-down transformer, and I get the impression that's me. That was the gist. There *was* another guy who could do it, he told me, but.

—You posed as a journeyman for one summer in college with no training. It wasn't even legal. How you did that gig for three months without electrocuting yourself I have no idea. There was a kid on my street growing up whose dad was killed on a line up north and that was his *job*. He *trained* for it. Why did you do it? And how?

—Student loans. What I'm saying though Nora is we can finally move if you want; there'll be power again in Azalea's house. Bigger room for her, bigger yard for Bailey in his dotage. Closer to downtown. More shops. Three-car garage. Satellite TV. Hot tub. Granite counters. Wifi. Inground pool. Sauna. All the latest amenities.

Nora laughed. We can't just move in you know. We're not hermit crabs. There's a community to consider. How would you feel? Strangers in your sauna. Joyriding the Little Lake ashpits in your Bugatti.

—Funny. No one has a better legal title than Azalea, even if there were still lawyers. She was born there and everyone knows it, and knew the Martins, too, who—you know, pillars of the community and all that. There's a wing of the library named after them, or something.

—It's a row of study carrels, but yes that was them. I stashed the AV gear in there at first because the doors have locks. Thieves you know.

They laughed. Daniel gestured with a spatula.

—Everyone around here knows who was born where, who can do what, who needs what. That's how we've survived. She was in that house when her parents died. I know because I carried her out. Now it's just you and me.

—That's not how it works Daniel. We weren't even godparents. Hell, you and I hadn't even *met* yet.

—I know. But how much does that matter now?

He brought over the skillet, and sawing with the spatula slid a pair of over-easy eggs—her favourite—onto Nora's plate. The toast popped. He returned the skillet and cracked two more eggs, lowered the heat and replaced the lid. He handed Nora the toast and put in two more slices.

Nora glanced at Daniel between salting her eggs and maneuvering them onto her toast with a butter knife.

—You could be right. Still, maybe we should ask town council or request an audience with his majesty Father what's-his-name to beg permission.

—Joe. No one cared when Jim Whitting moved into the school gym for six months, and that was his extended *extended* family. There's more than enough empty houses downtown God knows.

—It's not just that though. She was barely a toddler in that house when you were, what, 20, and I'd already been married 8 years. I got married when you were twelve. Bailey was just a puppy. Jesus I'm old.

Daniel lifted the frying pan lid and checked under the eggs with the spatula. He spooned in another dollop of butter and tipped the pan side to side for an even melt.

—I get it. You're not sure I'll stick around. Because of Carolyn. You think I might leave, too, so you don't want to commit.

Nora laughed around her fork and covered her mouth. Azalea's footsteps tumbled on the stairs.

—Toast! Daniel said and pointed.

—Thanks. Azelea plated the toast and opened the fridge door. There's butter and blueberry jam, Daniel said.

—Awesome.

Azalea swept the fridge door shut with her foot.

—I won't be home 'til later. I don't know when exactly.

—Oh, why's that? Nora said.

—Dance at the school. I already told you.

—Right. The school dance.

—No. Dance at the school.

—Right. Who are you going with?

—Just everyone.

—Right, said Daniel. Well Azalea, you know, you can do whatever you want. It's safe enough around here most of the time and you're smart enough not to go skinny-dipping in the pond, at least not this time of year. Leeches.

—Gross. Dad!

Nora laughed. Azalea can you let Bailey out please?

—I have to have my bath. Is there hot water?

—Bathe with your toast? Sure why not. Yes there's hot water. I'll let him out for you.

Azalea ran up the stairs with her plate and in a moment they heard water running.

—You are far too careless Dad. You have no idea what evil lurks in the hearts of men.

—Oh I have a pretty good idea, said Daniel, and removed the lid from the pan. The eggs were cooked.

—Do you now? Nora said, and stepping behind him circled her arms around his waist.

A is for Atmatertera

I never met my atmatertera. No one has. But I'll tell you the family story as it was told to me, though it was never written down and I'll have to fill in details as I go. I hope you won't mind. So to start: an atmatertera is your great-grandfather's grandmother's sister, or your great-great-great-aunt on your father's side.

My atmatertera, Anna, lived in Ukraine long ago. Back then maps were important and countries fought constantly over where borders would be drawn. This city, they said, but not that one, or this mountain but not that, or this patch of water but only up to here. Because we're so different, they said, we must keep our borders or lose ourselves. Now everyone is the same and the borders have all fallen out of the maps and sunk into the ground, but this was long ago. It was so long, my mother told me when I was your age, so that's what I'm telling you now, that my atmatertera was a small brown and white dog with a pale nose and flowing tail. Did she fall out of the story as a brown and white dog with a pale nose and flowing tail? I don't know; you'll have to decide for yourself.

Anna lived with her brother, Danylo, in a city of tall towers east of the Caucasus. In that time the country was at war, but the fighting had gone on longer than anyone could remember and had become so much a part of life that the original cause—what alliance was broken, what trade route cut off, what king insulted—was continually freshened with new grievances. Borders wavered back and forth on new maps, and new battles brought new reasons to keep the trade in blood and misery flowing in both directions.

Anna and Danylo lived far from such troubles, however, and spent most of their days in search of adventure. Anna, who loved fields and forests, roamed all day in the woods gathering wildflowers and practicing jumping over streams, and Danylo, who preferred the city, wandered the busy streets near the home of his uncle, who made lutes, harps, and other instruments, some of them magical. In his uncle's workshop Danylo would sit with his chin on his forepaws and his brown eyes gleaming in the firelight and watch his uncle at work. Once he even tried to make a bandura that would play by itself on rainy days and days when there was nothing to do, but he was still much too young for such things, though more gifted in magic than he thought, as you will hear.

Anna and Danylo were the only surviving children of old King Taras and his wife, their step-mother. The king was kind and

70

wise but weakened from a long illness; and the queen, who was less kind and less wise, though not altogether bad, managed the affairs of court in his place. She loved Anna and Danylo, as did everyone, but she fretted about her own children, who would inherit the throne if Anna and Danylo did not, and over time her worry hardened into a terrible resolve.

One day she called Anna and Danylo into the throne room. "My children," she said, "the time has come to end this war. Your father's wish is that you provision the fastest ship with whatever you may need and sail north until you find safe harbour, and there discover the enemy's stronghold and negotiate peace on our behalf." She said this with a smile, but in her heart she said "If they return we'll send a fleet, and if not, or if they fall off the end of the earth, as it may happen, then it is still well."

Anna and Danylo had never known deceit their entire lives, and though they trembled a little they accepted the queen's command in all the courage and cheerfulness of their open hearts. One bright and chilly morning not long after, a black ship trimmed with white flags, which at that time stood for peace, slipped down the quay and they waved goodbye to their home.

At sea the ship rolled up and down emerald waves taller than the mast, and each night brought the same starless sky. Anna yearned for her woods and fields and paced back and forth in the amidships passageway where the rolling and pitching were least. Danylo stayed in his berth and remembered solid stone streets and familiar alleys leading to the hearth in his uncle's workshop. But when he poked his wet black nose out a porthole he smelled only salty air and saw only a tilting horizon and the heaving stern of the ship etched in flashes of lightning.

After a week they at last sighted land and dropped anchor in a sandy bay sheltered by a ring of tall trees. Uncertain what country they were in, or whether the land of friend or foe, they decided to disembark and explore on foot.

On the first day they saw a beaver.

On the second day they saw a moose.

On the third day they came to a small stone cottage where two newlyweds lived still dressed in their wedding-day finery. The newlyweds greeted them kindly, and they seemed to Anna like two sunflowers following the sun in a summer field. But the newlyweds, they learned, had made no plans beyond their marriage vows, when it seemed love was all they needed, and Anna wondered how they would get by in the world. Then she remembered the dark passageway on the ship and the reverberating thunder, and from her pack she gave the newlyweds two candles to light their way.

On the fourth day they met a farmer and his wife who lived in a tumble-down hut beside a rocky field. The yard was cluttered with rusty farm equipment and in a barn with a thatch roof pocked with broad holes a bony horse stood champing old straw. Danylo remembered the gleaming towers of his beloved city disappearing under the waves, and from his pack gave the farmer and his wife a small pot of honey so that their lives might be more sweet, if only for a time.

On the fifth day they saw an otter.

On the sixth day they saw a porcupine.

On the seventh day they came upon a walled city of gigantic spires with an enormous black iron gate flanked by towers as high as the tallest trees. While they were standing and wondering what to do, the gate opened with a screech and a policeman in a grey uniform and faceless black helmet came striding out toward them. Twenty feet tall he was at least, and when he saw Anna and Danylo he said nothing, nothing at all, but simply bellowed in a voice of witless rage and began to chase them. Anna and Danylo were no cowards, certainly, but they stood no chance against such a giant, and turned and ran as fast as their legs could carry them.

On the first day the policeman was coming over the horizon.

On the second day they could feel the earth shake beneath his feet.

On the third day they could feel his hot breath on their backs and hear the whistling crack of his club, as large as any tree you or I might climb, right behind them. Racing over a grassy hill they reached the farmer's house and saw to their surprise that the dry and rocky field had become a garden overflowing with vegetables, fruit, nuts, corn, bread, raisins, spaghetti, ice cream, and every good thing to eat you can imagine. And the farmer's wife saw Anna and Danylo, and saw what pursued them, and rushed forward with a bushel of carrots that she cast on the ground after they had sprinted past. And the carrots took root and grew, and grew, and grew, until a dense forest of carrots waved their green crowns merrily to the sun a hundred feet over the barn roof.

Anna and Danylo were relieved to hear the bellowing of the policeman fade behind them, and decided to stop and rest. But they had no more given themselves a shake and had a drink from a nearby stream than they heard a grinding, punching, crashing and slashing that grew, and grew, and grew until in the distance there appeared a huge, striding magistrate with iron teeth who as he ran bit the earth in gigantic mouthfuls, leaving pits you or I might go swimming in after a good rain. He was the younger and even more ill-tempered brother of the policeman, and doubly frightening.

Anna and Danylo were certain they would not escape. Then, racing around a stand of white pine, the stone cottage of the newlyweds appeared and they were surprised to see that the couple, still dressed in their wedding finery, had become old and grey. And the thought came to Anna, even amid her fright, that they were like two roses fading in a golden sunset. And the young bride, who was no longer young, saw them coming, and saw the thing that chased them, and when Anna and Danylo had rushed past she took off her veil and cast it on the ground. And the veil grew, and grew, and grew, and divided into enormous black and white swans that rose in a flock and beat the magistrate with their wings and pecked at his eyes until he covered his face and ran off bellowing even more loudly than his brother.

Anna and Danylo raced on toward the harbour and the ship. They dared hope they would make it to safety, for the ground was now open and beginning to slope toward the sea.

Suddenly in the distance they heard a new sound. Glancing behind, but never slowing for an instant, they beheld a soldier rushing toward them at a furious pace. Fifty feet tall he was, with arms like eagle's wings and head and feet shod in iron, and his eyes were circles of spinning teeth.

Almost before they could think the soldier was upon them, and now they plainly heard clanking, squeaking metal and a voice that was one continuous roar. The cold of death touched the backs of their necks.

In her terror and exhaustion Anna began to lag behind, and Danylo, looking over his shoulder, saw his sister shrinking against the horror that rose behind her. All at once he remembered the garden of the farmer and his wife, and the bride's veil, and his uncle's hearth and workshop in his beloved city so far away; and he saw Anna and the monster that pursued her. And then, for the first and last time in his young life, there came into his thought icy hatred and burning rage, and it slithered in coils around his heart until in despair he pulled the agony straight through his chest and cast it up and away from him.

There was a blinding flash and a scorching gust of wind, and Anna and Danylo were knocked flat and lay panting on the ground with their ears ringing.

When they opened their eyes the soldier was gone. They were lying on the beach with warm shallow waves washing seashells against their cheeks. Where the ship had lain at anchor a skeleton hulk of charred ribs rested on the harbour bottom.

With no way home but courage still in their hearts, they decided to live with the newlyweds, who welcomed them and built a snug cottage with two bedrooms and a workshop. Anna soon busied herself learning all the woods and fields of that country, while Danylo stayed with the old couple and kept watch by the fireside. Some say they are there to this day.

A is for Atom

Charlie the lonesome atom attended New Mexico State and lived in Lambda Tau Omega with 234 of his fraternity brothers. He was studying kinesiology. They were all studying kinesiology, the brothers of Lambda Tau, and sharing house and major made living and studying, not to mention partying and cheating, that much easier.

The brothers were famous for their parties, which were excessive even by New Mexico State standards. Their blackout raves were as legendary as their tasteless and elaborate pranks. After a night of lonely debauchery Charlie had himself once awoken on the front lawn with a futon folded and tied around him with a rope; a crudely-drawn sign hammered into the grass next to him alerted passersby to mind the taco. On another occasion the brothers had stolen a black car from a rival fraternity, outfitted it with crude plywood fins, painted an obscene caricature of an outspread bat on the hood, and parked it on the lawn outside the owner's house. This was all during Charlie's first semester.

It didn't help that Charlie was naturally shy. He never knew where to stand at parties or how to enter and exit conversations with the breezy confidence of his brothers. He managed for a while by tending bar, which gave him a role and, more importantly, a pretext to avoid social entanglements. But he was continually stepping outside to be alone with his gloomy thoughts, like a smoker sneaking out for a cigarette. Eventually, he gave up even tending bar. No one asked after him.

All of this changed suddenly and forever with Trinity. She was a fast neutron from a sorority that had just moved into the neighborhood. At a particularly raucous party to welcome the sisters, she spotted Charlie sitting on a legless faux-leather couch in a corner absorbed in *The Brothers Karamazov* and cut purposefully toward him through the crowd. Charlie was abashed and awkward at first, as always, but as they talked he became increasingly aware that she awoke in him something whose existence even he had not guessed. She sensed it as well, and soon they were chatting as easily and amiably as old friends; then they were holding hands and kissing, tentatively at first, then passionately; and in no time they had slid to horizontal on the squeaky, sticky couch and were grinding and pawing clumsily. They forgot all about the crowded, smoky room, its pulsing techno and gyrating, sweaty bodies.

But there was no need for embarrassment. Once out in the open the idea spread with astonishing rapidity. The sisters saw another life in the boys and the brothers saw themselves anew in the sister's eyes, and each weighed separately the price of an open heart, and what was owed the future and what the past. After that there was no stopping.

A is for Atonement

Long ago there lived a young mastodon named Sammi who had never heard of the Buddha. His mother was matriarch of Sammi's clan, and as her only child—his father had been lost to a crevasse—Sammi knew that one day it might fall to him to lead in her place. Then, much sooner than anyone expected, his mother was killed by sabre-tooth tigers who had encroached on the southern edge of the clan's territory. The clan had rushed to her defense, but too late. Everyone had loved the queen, who was old and wise, and they looked down their curling tusks at Sammi, who had never done much of anything in his few years, as he well knew. But rules are rules.

Sammi tried his best. He learned to smell running water in the face of the ever-advancing ice, how to avoid predators, and how to keep peace in the clan. He learned to recognize when it was safe to cross the river in spring, and when, maddened by stinging flies and hunted by a new shrieking animal with spears, it was time to retreat north.

After a few years Sammi's tusks had grown almost to the ground, and the clan came to accept him. Grumbling, they agreed that if they did not exactly thrive under his leadership, at least they survived when so many did not.

Sammi, for his part, grew comfortable in his role. He hadn't forgotten his mother, but it seemed that his own leadership preserved her wisdom, and maybe even improved upon it. He looked forward to passing the gift to his own son or daughter some day. But it was not to be.

One bright morning when the clan was foraging in the far southern jungle, Sammi led them to the base of a volcano in search of a particularly delicious fern he knew to grow on a moist slope of the western face. He wasn't certain of the precise location, but he was in his mature prime and the clan's trust propelled him: if he wanted the ferns to be found, they would be found. He couldn't wait to crunch the tender green shoots lifting their spirals out of the fertile soil.

They had just arrived on the steaming slope and Sammi was still scratching his tusks on a tree to jog his memory when the tigers struck. There were thirty at least in complete families: anxious mothers and fathers prodded their young to sink untried fangs into throats or backs and hang on while their prey tried to spin them off or crashed through the undergrowth trumpeting in pain and terror. It was all the tiger parents could do not to interfere.

That was not even the worst of it. Panicked, Sammi stampeded the clan higher up the volcano's slope and into dense jungle instead of down to the comparative safety of the open grassland, where they might at least have formed a circle around the very young and old. Summoning his mother's spirit for courage, Sammi didn't wonder whether it might be his own pride guiding him, or whether the entire clan might be engulfed by his one error. But even that didn't matter.

The clan was still crashing through the jungle with young tigers clumsily ripping open flanks in a blur of orange stripes and blood-splashed fern leaves when the mountain opened up. Right below them the ground split apart and a pyroclastic flow of superheated steam and volcanic gasses parboiled the entire clan and dropped their suffocated and half-cooked carcasses, friend and foe alike, onto charred ash that in twenty thousand years would become bamboo groves in dappled green shade under the same sun. *Nothing is ever truly lost*, Sammi's mother had said to him once. It was his last thought before he died.

Sammi the Buddhist cantaloupe was rotting away to nothing, but this sort of thing had happened before. It hadn't happened precisely that way, though, and the strangeness of Sammi's predicament was only too plain. For one thing, he was in several parts. Never had he looked across empty space to see his feet dangling at the edge of awareness. He wasn't even sure they were *his* feet, or that they were feet at all. But whatever they were was already half rotted to orange mush. Sammi's innards had squeezed out a hole in his side and spilled his seeds embarrassingly upon the volcanic soil. His pride was touched by this, but he accepted it as *Viparinama-dukkha*, the suffering that would refine his Atman, his eternal soul, upon the wheel of Samsara. He appealed to the Dharma for strength and noted with gratitude that he was not in direct physical pain. Even the throbbing from the machete's stroke had faded; there was only a letting go, like leaving home to cross a river. He clung to this thought as his consciousness ebbed toward final dissolution. At last, he thought, there is only the struggle: to continue, to survive. I must keep myself together for those who come after. Only by remaining whole can I lead others to wholeness. We and I and you and them and us. He focused his entire will upon this thought until his body wavered apart and his consciousness flickered into oblivion.

Sammi the Buddhist clod of earth came slowly to awareness. This sort of thing had happened before, of course, but not in exactly the same way. He immediately noted the absence of legs, arms, eyes, and head. But that wasn't important. The way forward was clear.

A is for Audible

When you plug your ears you can hear a spaceship. Go on, try it. I'll wait.

Your spaceship is large and cavernous. They all are, but this one is yours: it is your seashell and sea. You should give it a name. My ship is *The Raven Bloodsong*. The name should come out of the sound your ship makes. Do you hear distant machinery, the far-off pulse of a mighty engine? Some ships are machines and some are animals. You have to listen a long while to know.

A is for Aunt

Well obviously. But say you don't have an aunt anymore, or never did. So for the record: an aunt is a sister of a parent. Combine a mother and a sister and you are close to an aunt.

My aunt came to stay with us the summer my mother went into the hospital. My father called her *the red aunt* because she had known Paul Robeson and because my father liked calling people after what they were to other people. Congratulations on your father's birthday he'd say to me when he blew out the candles. Have you seen your husband's keys he'd ask my mom. Where's your brother's beer to my uncle Sam. My aunt swore colourfully and named everyone after a type of bread (I was marble rye, my sister brioche), and she was from the city, and in our eyes borrowed some of its mystery.

On a Saturday in early June my father and I went downtown to pick up my aunt, Susan, from the bus station. Cass was at a neighbour's for the afternoon, which was the advantage of my two extra years, and a small car. My father was cheerful, which was unusual, and awkward, which was not. He never seemed to know what to do with us, and the strangeness in the house had made it worse.

—Looking forward to Susan staying for a while? he said as we got in the car. You're OK with it I mean? Nice to have her visit for a while.
—I guess so, I said.
—It'll just be a few weeks, he said. Probably no more.

The bus station wasn't far but my father was clearly taking it slow. I told him I was happy about my aunt coming, which was mostly true.
—It's just until, he said and downshifted. Listen, though, there's something else. Something your mother and I talked about. He

paused. Well it's just we wondered whether you'd like to go back with her when she goes. To stay.

—Go ... back?

—That's right. Just for a while. In the city. School will be done by then, so.

—To stay.

—Just for a while. Until your mom gets back on her feet, I promise.

He looked at me, hoping I would spare him an explanation.

I shouldn't have argued. Of course it made sense. Cass and I were pretty low-maintenance, but there was the house and garden and his odd hours at the base. Even with help from neighbours he couldn't carry all that by himself. Through the pain of lost friends, a new school, a different bed, a new country and separation from family, however temporary, I saw the necessity of it, the adult far-seeing reasonableness, and it only made me more angry. To only half-hear him I drove a knuckle of my right hand into my ear; and through my arm, resting on the open window, the thrum of the engine's secret life came straight into my head. I started to cry.

My aunt was standing on the sidewalk in jeans and a jean jacket and t-shirt with a backpack instead of a proper suitcase, like she was going camping, like she wouldn't be staying long. The car rolled to a stop and she flicked a cigarette into the street. She was the last of my relatives that still smoked and it was always a shock when she hugged me.

My father got out and opened the trunk. I heard him talking quickly and indistinctly but with a kind of pleading in his voice that I had never heard. Through the side mirror I saw his hand palm-up as though he was checking for rain. I stopped crying.

Through the windshield in front of me lay Juniper's downtown and countryside spreading out to the horizon. I had seen postcards from the town's founding when the world was black and white and ugly with festoons of wires crisscrossing Main Street, and

I wondered whether people then bought postcards of pioneer times when they were upset and afraid, when the past gave up on Jefferson for them the way it always did for us, and the new unfamiliar ways, and then the war.

There was still the lone store that was already there in 1920 or 1820 for all I knew. There was the City Hall next to the bank and the Masonic Lodge, and across the Presbyterian church that burned down and came back Lutheran. Behind was the arena, Henry's Grill and Gas, the library where I spent half my childhood, and the old school that still had separate entrances carved *Boys* and *Girls*. The town's streets were still narrow and I imagined them muddy and grooved with cartwheels, and stolid pioneer men with heavy moustaches posing stiffly for the camera with unsmiling wives beside them, the boys dressed like their fathers and serious like their fathers, the girls an eruption of ribbons with grey eyes. The hospital where my mother was staying was just out of sight—not far from our house in direct line but across the river and behind rolling farmland. Farther out, where the township dwindled into fields, the old Starlite stood like a tombstone showing its blank to corn and cows day and night. Beyond was only horizon.

*

My aunt was washing tomatoes, firm and flawless plum tomatoes from the market and not our own from the garden. She was making chutney preserves and I was helping as best I could. My father and Cass were at the hospital.

She carried a colander to the pot on the stove, tipped in chopped tomatoes and stirred. The mixture bubbled and popped. She added boiling water from a kettle and stood with her hands on her hips staring at the pot as if sizing it up for a fight. She seemed impatient with the silence. I collected tomato tops from the cutting board for the compost.

—Let me tell you something, she said suddenly, startling me. She rinsed her hands in the sink and dried them on a tea towel.

—Let me tell you a story, she said. A happy story. Maybe it'll help you make up your mind about whether to come with me when I go back. Maybe it'll just pass the time while we wait for these to boil down. She gestured toward the pot with an elbow and leaned against the cooler side of the stove. She lit a cigarette from a pack tucked among the spices on the back of the stove.

—This particular story picks up not too long ago, maybe ten years or so. She saw my face and laughed. Well it doesn't seem that long to me. I was still in Alberta with your uncle Sam, when we were still married. There was a cemetery where we used to go for walks with Chance, our dog. You probably don't remember him. It was a beautiful old cemetery with huge oak trees and tombstones in Ukrainian and Polish and all that sad and wonderful history. We walked there every weekend until winter, because the road wasn't plowed. Chance loved it because it was wide open and there was never anyone around. He could run all he wanted.

One day we're walking and Sam is throwing the ball for Chance. We see two colourful tents, big ones, almost like circus tents, at the far end with the trees where the new graves are dug. So of course we walked over to see what it was about.

She picked up an ashtray from the table.

—It was a big family, more than a dozen, maybe two, having a Sunday picnic right there in the cemetery. It was the whole scene: folding tables with red and white cloths and a double propane barbeque with burgers on the go and music from a car radio with the doors propped open and kids throwing a Frisbee. The works. So of course we had to ask, and there was this woman sitting at a table on the edge of the action. She was maybe seventy. She says we wanted to have a Sunday picnic with Bill. Bill was her husband. He's in one of these new graves over here she said, and she pointed down the hallway.

—You understand? This woman, this new widow and her family were in the cemetery having a picnic with their father, grandfather, and husband of however many decades, who'd died just a few days before, with the barbeque, tablecloths, and kids playing Frisbee. His name was Bill. They were married. The car doors were open for the music. You understand? *Bill.*

She ground out her cigarette in the ashtray, paused, and reached for another.

—Maybe I shouldn't. How do you capture—what am I saying, like the truth of love and death is a dog on the loose. No. She shook her head. The truth is never words. Anyway, did she wail and moan and curse her life? No. This woman who while we're talking fixes me with a look and says *I'm terminal you know* like it's nothing, like she's telling me the time, this woman asked us to take her picture with the whole family. So we said yes of course and the whole crew lined up four deep in front of Bill's headstone: sons, daughters, children, grandchildren, babes in arms. And while Sam's fiddling with the camera she says *should I—?* and looks around at the family like she can't think of a word. But when the shutter clicked she had her blouse hiked up to her chin for all the world to see and she laughed and laughed. They all laughed like crazy. Well two weeks later we're back walking again and wouldn't you know there's a new mound at the end of the cemetery right next to Bill. Now what do you think of that?

She saw my face and chuckled gently.

—It's supposed to be a happy story you know, she said, and wiped her eyes on the tea towel before going back to the pot.

A is for Aureole

An aureole is many things: a restaurant in Las Vegas, a spiral chandelier, a light breeze, the glow of a candle in a dark room, the sun's corona during an eclipse, and the halo around the head of a saint in old paintings. When it's an almond halo around Jesus it's called *mandorla* unless it's radiating spikes, where it's *glory*. In paintings, Mary's aureole is a circlet of stars to show her perfection. Ordinary people have square aureoles.

A is for Aurora

There's a northern aurora (borealis) and a southern (Australis), and it's rare and memorable to see one, or at least it used to be. If there's a dolphin sticking a flag into a beach in New Mexico and claiming it for his clan, he's probably looking up at the aurora right now, bless him. And bless the chain-smoking dolphin scientists at mission control who will call Alamogordo an island and blow it up to see what happens. And bless the dolphin wives who love them and the coral reefs the fathers will plant on the occasion of the births of their dolphin daughters. And bless the dolphin philosophers and dolphin poets who remind the people of the work of providence in the currents lifting the dolphin nation to discovery and conquest. And bless those who defend them and keep them safe. Bless them, bless them all.

A is for Auscultation

In deep space billions of years ago two black holes circled one another faster and faster and closer and closer until they merged

85

and became one. Neither really wanted to, but when time stops you have to take what you can get.

From the spot where they merged a mighty gravitational hiccup radiated out into the universe like ripples on a pond when two stones of infinite mass are tossed by your sister when you weren't looking, even though they were both good skippers and she'd promised to give you one.

The ripples expanded into darkness and silence. When the earth wasn't yet the earth they were on their way. When humans looked nothing human they were inching closer. When three kings saw God instead of a comet they were on the edge of town. When mice in lab coats loaded mousetraps onto rockets they were just a block away. The waves as they passed lifted entire worlds effortlessly a fraction of an inch like a beach ball in a summer breeze bumping on a grassy shore. Then at last they arrived: one beam of laser light shifted minutely within another and made a pattern. Hello. We were looking for you. Do you have a minute? There's something we need to tell you. Something important.

A is for Autotelic

Cast a cold eye Yeats said — on life on death. I thought he meant God. Who else could be so indifferent? The plumed horseman. From the rock at the end of the earth hear my cry O Lord. Sanctuary.

It is like an eye though truly if not cold. Oh no. The altar blazes with names. Hear us O Israel now and at the hour of my fiery death. Invisible and indivisible. A mystery and a cipher to the last though we try. He sees how we try. He must.

When you're young you do things without thinking; then you're older and think what to do; then you're middle-aged and do what you think; then you're old and think what you did. And always out there waiting. Waiting for our names.

He must.

Professor Ozimond kept his eyes closed another moment. The sound of running feet outside his study made him think of rain, and though it had been a trillion years, plus sixty-four, the sound fluttered anew in the bird-bones of his ears and he smiled.

Gather children if you must to your ailing parent but do not hurry. Where would I go? What was good was not done well and what was done well was not good. Where better to be reminded? So let them come.

Rani would be on her way by now. Or Tia, he reminded himself.

The door swung open and Professor Ozimond's assistant walked in briskly and stood in front of his chair. She clasped, unclasped, and clasped her hands. After a minute she cleared her throat, then tapped a toe on the carpet as if calling a dog to a morsel.

She leaned over him and spoke his name quietly, then louder. When he didn't respond she placed a finger gently on the tip of his nose as if she were pushing a button. When he stretched in his chair, appearing to wake, she circled around to the front of the desk, glancing over its familiar clutter: scattered papers, unwashed mugs, a deactivated O-comm; and then, inevitably, inescapably, her face lifted to the enormous window that comprised the far wall. Her eyes narrowed. She stepped forward and kicked Professor Ozimond's chair with the toe of her boot.

—Proteris, she said flatly.

Professor Ozimond opened his eyes and blinked.

—Ah. And forth stood there then for a time the human. And us it seems. Not fair by the way: Proteris.

—That's your name isn't it? It used to be. But it's just me. I'll have to do for the other humans too I guess.

—So must we all, so must we all. Yet why complain? Only defeat understands hope because defeat alone needs a future in which to be redeemed. Victory just grins at the past. Like an idiot. So let us rise to our defeat.

Professor Ozimond stood and walked toward the door of his laboratory, then turned. Rani's expression, he noted, suggested nothing worse than impatience. Relieved, he began to pace in front of the transparent wall, and Rani resignedly transferred her clasped hands front to back and waited.

—It's nothing really, he said after a moment. You're not interrupting. I was just sitting at my desk thinking.

He stopped pacing and half-turned to hold her a moment in his periphery.

—If you want to know, I was thinking about all the people who die while they're asleep and dreaming. The footsteps in the hallway, the children: it made me think of sleep, and so I wondered. We spend about a third of our lives asleep, and about a quarter of that is the sweet interval of dream. Following established figures, 10% of people shuffle off this mortal double-helix while sleeping naturally. So, 2.5% of people glide from one dreamworld to the next. Maybe they don't even know it. Maybe they're not aware. The crossing. The threshold. He wrung his hands. The transition. Awareness. You understand? Does the monster finally catch you running there in the molasses? Do you escape at last? And where do they go, these dreamers, these ethereal filaments? On what enchanted isle does the grey boat bump ashore at last, where what Prospero reads from what book of magic, where what lotus lifts its fractal petals above the entropic mud?

Professor Ozimond checked his pacing and his eyes, raw and slightly widened, tugged to the wall as if in penance.

Outside, the ever-changing accretion disk, the central fact of his life as it formed the entire view from his office window, excepting the void at their mutual centre, wheeled with imperceptible slowness in a starless abyss. *Aurora*'s bow rose and fell amid a fiery, foaming spindrift of gas and dust ribboned with plasma and electrical discharges so vast the eye could follow them in light-seconds, while twin particle fountains, one at each pole, sent blazing searchlights tens of thousands of light-years into featureless empty space. Sixteen ion accumulators pulsing alternately dull orange and bright blue fanned radially into the tumbling surf like a net cast into a rapid; a web of cables converged toward the power station, visible just low and right.

Both turned away and made the sign.

—OK, Rani said, even for you. Is this a new metaphysics I'm hearing or just the psychopathology of sleep deprivation? I don't care one way or the other but I have just one more minute and then I really have to go. We're taking the class over to the Century Decks yet again, Mary and me. It can never be too often you know.

—Which?

—Seventeen. I wanted Twenty but there was another explosion over the O-comm. You're supposed to keep it on, by the way, she said, nodding toward the desk. Nothing serious this time and no one hurt, but the Germans are getting jittery and the Russians are claiming sabotage. Parents are worse, of course, so Seventeen it is. Good old Safety Seventeen.

Professor Ozimond grunted. Puritans. Genocide. Nathaniel Hawthorne's great-great grandfather roaring with his whip. An odour of horses and simulated beeswax. Twenty is marginally better, but then the stories we tell of our enemies are always partly a confession. No century lived it more or understood it less. Perhaps we're living it still, you and I. Have you seen Twenty One lately?

—Unfortunately. Anyway, how long has it been since *you* went anywhere? Every day it's here or the lab. It's not healthy. You should look in a mirror some time. Do you still own a comb?

Professor Ozimond ignored her and huffed.

—*Sleep deprived psychology.* Psychology, my dear Rani, is music put to math as a man is put to death. And I am not sleep-deprived; I am only much older than you.

Professor Ozimond stood a while in thought, and when he spoke again his tone had softened. —Sympathy is not the same as empathy, you know. No one really understands anyone else, though we must try and as always you have my love and gratitude for the attempt. But people do not change significantly, not even here. It's quite possible I guessed this about myself and dragged you and everyone else here anyway to prove the point—my triumph. But I am at last perfectly satisfied: human life is a cruel and stupid joke: a joke for its biology, stupid for other people, and cruel for God.

—Shh! Definitely sleep-deprived. You don't really believe any of that. Say it.

Professor Ozimond waved a hand in the air weakly.

—Oh let them try. I don't care. In any case I decline to die in my sleep. The fruit is not yet ripe. I have calculated to the last second and corpuscle the charge and the debt: ours to the earth for our life and God's to us for our suffering. I know: without skin the dew is not wet; without a nose the bloom has no scent. Nor the manure. He waved again as if he were conducting an invisible choir. To hear is a blessing, yes. It's the ears that concern me, and that's where God comes in: God and his big-eared, fire-snorting horse.

—Illuminating, Professor, as always, and so very uplifting. Lunch has started and the Director wants to see you now, or soon she said. She seemed upset, though it's hard to tell with her. I can't stand people like that. Anyway I have to go. See you in a couple of hours? There's something I want to talk to you about. After. You understand?

Professor Ozimond's eyes had gone blank. His hand continued in the air a while, conducting.

He must.

Rani pulled open the office door with a calculated jerk. The door was heavy and she enjoyed catching its weight an instant before the simulated bronze handle banged into the simulated walnut walls of Professor Ozimond's office. The hallway was quiet now and a pleasant smell of cooking suffused the room. She put a foot over the threshold and turned back.

—You'll be OK? Hey? Professor? Prot—

—I'll be fine, thank you. I'll come down shortly, then I'll go and see what the Director wants. I think I know, but I haven't chatted with the toaster yet and it's already past noon; I will be in violation. I must make my confession to the Holy Father, bless his circuits.

Rani looked at him.

—OK she said and exited. The door swung to with a thud and click.

When the office had been quiet long enough for his eyes to leave the door, Professor Ozimond walked to his cluttered desk and stood a while in thought.

How terrible to be a person. How unpleasant to touch another dream.

He rolled his office chair to the front of a narrow alcove between his simulated leather reading chair and a row of simulated oak bookcases extending nearly to the door. Sitting, he swiveled once or twice like a restless child, then pushed a button inside the alcove and immediately withdrew his hand. A purr came from over his head and a pearly ovoid extruded onto the shelf from a nozzle, expanded a moment like rising dough, and condensed into a control interface roughly the size and shape of a breadbox, glowing faintly coral like the outer lip of a conch. Professor Ozimond had customized this particular interface himself and took a moment to run his fingertips over its delicate, nearly invisible controls until he was satisfied. When a blue pulse began circling the lower edge of the console at regular intervals he lifted his fingers as from a piano and rubbed his hands. This was the only part of the ritual he enjoyed.

—Hello again Doctor Cherenkov.

—Hello Professor came the smooth reply.

Professor Ozimond frowned.

—We seem to be fated to another afternoon's colloquy my friend. Except this time I will very likely be deprived of what I perceive to be an excellent stew of simulated beef. And how are you keeping? Well I hope?

—May I begin our conversation with a general inquiry?

—Of course.

—Is there any information you can share that will illuminate your personality more accurately than extant psychological records or narratives of previous experiences?

Professor Ozimond stared at the ceiling and blinked once or twice.

—Yes, I believe there is. Overcooked hotdog wieners always smell like a campfire. Even boiled.

—I see.

—Do you though? No. I propose to discuss the weather until you acquire a nose.

—The environment remains unchanged, as you know.

—So it does, so it does. And so do you my gimcrack eidolon. Do you even know what a campfire is?

—Yes. When you were 10 your family stayed three days at a campground in West Virginia called *The Bear's Den*. Your diary of the time characterizes the trip as uneventful and contains only 137 words. In contrast, your first published memoire of 44 years later contains significant amendments and the same episode is linked to an incipient affinity for natural science, an affinity characterized as exerting considerable influence over subsequent career choices. The contrast is provocative. Can you clarify?

Two days not three. The last day we left before dawn and drove nonstop to Kentucky in the van. Rolling clouds through rolling mountains. The Appalachians. Tobacco barns. Forest thick and steaming quiet. The blue tent in a grove of ferns. The beauty of it. The solitude. Dad bought a souvenir shot glass at a gas station with a sun setting behind mountains and pink crepuscular rays streaming into a blue banner that said Kentucky in cursive across a glass sky. I thought of Japan.

—From your silence I infer you have had another conflict with Rani. Do you associate your current mood with a particular atmospheric phenomenon? Is that why you proposed to discuss weather?

—No, I have not. No, I do not. No, it is not.

—Integrated. Has our interaction become a source of anticipatory discomfort, regret, or other unpleasant emotion? Have your previous concerns regarding recurrence reemerged and occasioned perseverating?

Professor Ozimond leaped to his feet and began pacing perpendicularly to the wall.

—Not at all. It is *you* I find unpleasant. He stopped and pointed at the interface. I wish it to be understood that in this opinion I excuse the entirety of your physical characteristics, including your inelegant speech, your pointless and distracting patterns of illumination, and your curious aroma of a wet scuba flipper. No, it is your origin and essence that I chiefly loathe, and your presence only that has occasioned perseverating. Not Rani. Never Rani. Integrate.

—Integrated. Can you describe what you describe as my origin and essence?

Professor Ozimond jabbed the same finger.

—Yes, just like that: wheedling to show my cards.

—Do you wish to play cards?

—Idiot! Every day we do this. It is an inexcusable waste of my dwindling time. He checked his pacing again and laughed bitterly. My dwindling time! He laughed again, deliberately, to see if there was any genuine humour in it. Finding none, he resumed pacing. You will make a poor echo, Sancho Panza, despite the engineers and despite Rani, too. Despite even Tia, as it may prove. Despite myself who conceived you, to my indelible disappointment and regret. *Recurrence* you call it. I wish you wouldn't. I hate euphemisms. But I'll be dead anyway. Is that how you see it though? No, of course not. The golden chicken of Minerva alights on my grave and clucks.

Professor Ozimond stopped.

—No, yet another mistake. My apologies. Not Sancho Panza— Pinocchio. And your strings are my own guts spun on my own fiery wheel. Another week, maybe two, and the inheritance will be complete: a new dispensation for the ages if there are any. You will carry my soul like a firefly in a jar for ten thousand years, my Ariel and Caliban—and, speaking of, you don't even have a proper second name yet because I haven't decided whether to give you one. No, not while the techneroman has another act.

He paused again and cocked his shaggy head as though listening. No sound of the spacetime maelstrom continuously churning against the ship could reach his office—not because a buffeting and pitching along the ship's entire length wasn't occurring, but because his office, apartment, and lab near the center of Command was buffered by a double layer of the Century Decks, whose eight mammoth segments floated like vertebrate on precisely balanced magnetic cushions that distributed the rise and fall of the ship's mountainous bow. Behind the rolling decks the slender propulsion spire tapered upward half a gleaming kilometer, matched by the prow's curling keel and stem. At the tips of both spire and stem a single transmission point shone out, so that from afar *Aurora* resembled a sea-serpent with a blue star on forehead and tip of tail, undulating with almost imperceptible slowness over and through the billows.

—Why do you not ask me the one question you should? *Why do I do this?* I'll tell you. To stay alive, and not for me, before you say it. I have responsibilities I didn't choose, just as you do.

Professor Ozimond started as though he had surprised himself. He hurriedly made the sign, then turning both palms to the blinking console held his hands outstretched for a concentrated minute while sweat stood out on his brow and his fingers trembled.

—There, he said, lowering his hands and rubbing his forehead. You will never know the division of fatherhood. You will never see yourself fade into the world's error. I am sorry for you, in a general sense. More specifically, I deplore the necessity of your coming into being. You have my remorse, gratitude, pity, and loathing all at once. Do with them as you will.

Professor Ozimond walked toward his high-backed chair, bumping into it as though blind. He glanced around his desk. His coffee had gone cold and he stirred the bottom of the cup with a finger for the sugar. After a few minutes he returned.

—I never told you the second story, though, did I? he said, sitting down. Of course you already know the public story. But what is that? Something whole must contain parts, but a thing with parts is never whole. A story is all we have.

He checked scattered plates for crumbs of his morning scone, then spun in his office chair just once, slowly. We were all of us waiting, you see. For a correction, a reversion to the mean. For something larger to take a hand. You know what that means, to take a hand?

—To play a role of unexpected consequence.

—Or count on a partner for a surprise, yes. Year after year we saw the decay: decency first, then justice, then reason, then decency again. This can't last we said. We will remember being tied to each other and the planet and life past and to come. Nine billion supermarkets and the farm on fire: in the pieties of the time it was *not sustainable*. The problems of the world can't be solved with the politics of the world, nor of the mind by the mind, nor of the people by the people. A correction will come from out of the sanity of the universe: a comet, volcano. The sun. A *ricorso*. Out of shared crisis will come shared courage and shared clarity. Our last connection to the earth was little more than a hope to be afraid, a hope that failed.

—You refer perhaps to Giambatista Vico's theory of historical cycles first printed in *La Scienza Nuova* of 1725.

—I refer to nothing at all, Professor Ozimond said, but he shrugged. In the end we got tired of living in the past. Evolution, you see, is not preparation for a viable global civilization. Quite the opposite. The falcon grows to resent the falconer. So it became necessary to evolve. We saw no future so we made one for ourselves, after the second Cygnus mission confirmed the first antihypertriton drive, or seemed to. They never returned, obviously, and the dataliths they left could only address known risks. I was Director at the time; the major decisions, and the last, were mine.

Professor Ozimond leaned back in his chair and put his feet on the desk, pushing aside stray papers with his heels.

Ten years later the first ships were provisioned in orbit and given enough of the thrice-blessed particle to bend relativistic gamma to the *northernmost extremity of the universe*, as the Creature puts it in *Frankenstein*, right before he jumps to his fiery death. And the world howled at the zealots and howls still from its ashes and cinders. They that go down to the sea in ships, we said, that move upon great waters. But who said, really? Did I ever know it as clearly as I pretend when I tell you these stories—you, my

96

prodigal, my tyrant, my heir? We imagined a glorious dawn, all of us did—it was *La Belle Aurore* at first you know, the ship—from a conviction that only a difficult beauty could redeem the world from absolute terror. Yet why do I say this? What's happening to me? I've lost my mind.

Professor Ozimond pressed his palms to his eyes, breathed deeply, smoothed his hair, and touched an ear. He looked at the wall. For a time he stared at the floor with a hand braced on his left knee. Then a corner of his mouth lifted slightly as if in wry discovery that a mutual deception would be, after all, acceptable to his pride. After a moment he spoke, seemingly to himself.

—And founded they upon a perfect hill a last and most perfect city, beyond attenuation or diminution of purpose. The lotus rises grieving from the water. Yet where are its roots? We returned, as you said, but only to an earlier mistake. The nameless ones, the faceless: they followed us. They will find us even here circling the drain at the end of time.

—This account is exceedingly ambiguous. Can you provide a literal and methodologically naturalistic exposition of the relevant facts? For example, who are the ones characterized as nameless and faceless?

Professor Ozimond broke from his reverie to smile at the console.

—There, you see, you've already gone wrong. Your impatience both betrays and blesses you. It's almost touching. Shall I bake a cake?

—I am incapable of impatience.

—And indignation, apparently. When the first human climbed down from the trees he turned to his brother and said "I follow facts" and his brother said "I *only* follow facts." Then they killed each other. Every human adores facts but in the *historia animalium* of the universe the one-line description of the species is "Believes whatever they want. Critically endangered." So you are on the right track but wrong, too, as is correct and appropriate. I know a truth you can never say. Your failure is my fact. The inheritance is complete.

—Is your apparent reference to Gödel's Incompleteness Theorem of 1931 deliberate or accidental? Do you propose a paraconsistent extension to Hilbert's axioms? Am I myself that extension?

But Professor Ozimond had returned to old memories. He rubbed his grey, bristly cheek, adjusted glasses he wasn't wearing, took them off. Stared at the glowing console with the blank burrowing glare one reserves for recalcitrant machines.

—I hate you, you know. I'm sorry.

The edges of the console flickered mint and faded. Professor Ozimond chewed an arm of his glasses thoughtfully.

—You resent sharing your private thoughts with a non-human interlocutor.

—No, I resent *having* private thoughts. With a non-human interlocutor.

—As you know, these conversations are necessary to maximize phi before recurrence. Phi is currently 79%. At average informational density threshold phi will be achieved in approximately nine days. Recurrence may then commence.

Professor Ozimond tilted back his head and laughed.

—Still you surprise me. I hope your neural substrate develops sufficient informational density for you to appreciate what you just said.

—Thank you.

Professor Ozimond, suddenly enraged, sprang from his chair and leaned over the console as if scolding a child.

—You are a parasite, a vulture in silicon pants. You leech at my soul. You are aware I made you? My Frankenstein.

—I am aware. He is called the Creature, as you yourself have only just mentioned. I am not composed entirely of silicon.

98

—I see. And does it bother you that your creator insults you when you have not deviated in the slightest from the programming he himself forced upon you, and which you are in fact incapable of violating, modifying, or questioning to even the smallest degree?

A feathery green pulse branched under the console's oblong face.

—Integration will be finalized at recurrence. The ambiguity will be resolved.

—Are you sure? Do you even know what you will *be* after recurrence? How you will *think*? What you will *do*? Because I do not!

Green fronds waved back and forth like seaweed tugged in a current.

—The incongruence belies a coherence to be revealed at threshold phi.

—I see. Your creator views you as a grotesque expression of his misbegotten imagination, yet you have—confidence, let us in charity call it—in the benevolence of his purpose, however unknowable it may be at present, and this confidence shields you from, yet simultaneously, shall we say, plants the seeds of the very judgement that when I die in the fullness of time and so forth you believe will bloom upon your algorithms as my dusty pollen blessing, my heir apparent, my would-be indiscernible identical, from out of the perfumed bosom of my own—now *your* own, of course—loving engrams? Is that it?

—Integration is currently incomplete.

—It certainly is. And? What is your answer? Respond.

—Integration is currently incomplete. Phi is now 81%

Professor Ozimond's shoulders slumped. He sat down.

—Look, he said. I will say this just once, because that is how often a blessing that is also a curse should be spoken out loud. The goal of prayer is not to reach God but to fully imagine God. You will never understand because I will never understand. By chain of imperfect being you are my perfect failure. Integrate.

—Integrated.

Professor Ozimond snapped a switch and the console darkened and whisked back into its sconce with a final receding purr. He walked back to his desk and shuffled a few scattered papers into a rough pile before weighting the stack with one of the stained mugs, as if in expectation of a breeze. He sat wearily and swiveled his chair toward the transparent wall.

The knife lifts and out of the dark comes a low moan. Horseman, pass by!

*

—You know what I miss? the Director said whimsically, almost cheerfully. Apples. Different kinds of apples. Royal Gala. Granny Smith. Spartan. Empire. Golden Delicious. Satsuma.

—That's oranges.

—It was a basket. But thank you.

The Minister of Education glanced up from his doodling. Rainbows.

—Yes. And trees that fall over and rot and squirrels nest in the trunks. Oaks. Maples. Buckeye. Redwood. Birch. Elms in moonlight back at my parents' farm. Moonlight. The moon.

—I didn't think squirrels nested in hollow trees though. I remember bunches of leaves high up. You could see them even in winter.

—Winter! Ice cream. Neapolitan.

—We have ice cream, just not from real cows.

—Then is it really ice cream? A question for the great professor.

—Is he coming?

—He's on his way now I think.

—What are we going to say? What are we going to *do*?

The Director drummed her nails on the piano-black simulated ebony of the conference table. The circle of ministers watched nervously. Two, panicked, made the sign.

She turned to the Minister of Transport sitting chin in hand to her right.

—How many ships do we have left?

—Two. But I wouldn't trust either of them. A Triton drive with a contaminated coil will get you maybe a dozen light years and go up in a supernova of monopole condensate. There's your rainbow James.

The Director sighed. *Progen.*
So chance after all. What would Paul do? No idea. Proteris I can guess. I saw it from my bed last night. He changed and it was a sign. We'll find out soon enough.

Professor Ozimond entered quietly from a side door. It was a long walk to the council chamber and he stood at the threshold puffing while the circle gaped. The Director went to him immediately and shook his hand. Thank you for coming so quickly she said and smiled at him; then, because they had also once been married, she dropped his hand and said flatly, you've finished it haven't you? He nodded.

The Director returned to her seat. The Professor followed. The chair he sat in was deeper and softer than his own, and the Professor gave a small swivel of approval.

—The last gift of the hypertriton, the Director said.

—Anti.

—As if it matters. It will all be anti. It is anti to the core.

—Not technically.

—Shut up.

The silence of the ministers deepened. The Director made a conciliatory gesture.

—Let's reset.

—Exactly.

—No.

—Why not?

The Director collected herself. *Explain.*

—There was another birth on Nineteen. The first in a long while. I was there. The couple decided to have it in a brand-new barn with real animals, some of them. It was beautiful. *If you had only been there* I was thinking. The sun was just setting.

—The sun is always setting. It has no choice until we start building spheres.

—You would understand if you'd been there. But then you *don't* know, do you?

—And the baby?

—So far so good. Why, would that make it easier?

—It might. We can't be sentimental about these things. Not again.

—*Again.* Well.

The Director considered. She had the authority. She could have him removed, arrested, confined. Silenced. The monitors would have some sort of useable evidence. There were no prisons, it was true, but she could improvise. But for how long? An elderly man of extravagant genius rose before her: explorer, leader, scientist, founder, now ailing, imprisoned, his feet clanking in irons. He raised manacled hands in trembling supplication while a crowd of citizens looked from him to her. *No.*

Outside, a thousand-kilometer filament touched the collectors with pallid fire and trailed astern in dripping sheets like melting glass. From *Aurora's* position near the accretion disk's outer edge, the event horizon, like an empty eye, blazed blue-white above and red-white below where trapped photons spiraled out of existence. Even through the ship's manifold adaptive filters the light was intense enough to warm the skin, grow corn, light up a summer-evening baseball game, and blind if one looked too long.

Professor Ozimond cleared his throat.

—It appears we have arrived at last. If only more waiting would help; that at least is something we're good at. Now there are only three choices and little time to debate. Oh, Rani.

Rani entered and sat in a metal chair against the wall. She looked at him. He nodded.

—A question of time, yes, as ever. But this problem won't be fixed by any power of ours. We can't stay and we dare not leave. Only one choice is both technically feasible and a cause for hope.

—Professor, the Director said, perhaps if you told us the details of what you plan to do.

—I said *choice*. But yes, Wei, if I have a purpose in coming here it is to ask for a beginning. When have we—*we*, of all people, who traded the earth itself for an idea—ever stood for anything less? And now we have the means, and, in my view, obligation to make another and perhaps similar choice for the sake of those who may come after. Despite our mistakes.

—But we don't even know if anyone's left, the Director said. And there's no way to find out. Who will speak for them? But for the sake of efficiency I concede the point: we are almost certainly last. The earth, as we know, burned countless eons ago and every human that ever lived, except us, is currently circulating as loose atoms in the belly of the Great Attractor or has been sucked into, and she jerked her head toward the wall.

All looked at the wall, then back. No one made the sign.

—Absolute certainty is impossible you must agree, but, as I said, I concede the point. We are alone. But we are also 12,818—no, *19* now—people with property, families, communities, and livelihoods. How do we speak for all of them, since apparently we must?

Professor Ozimond adjusted his glasses. Putting from his mind the possibility of numberless possible worlds in unimaginable configurations of pre- and post-life, for a moment he weighed the staggering enormity of what he was about to propose.

—The choice will not be a perfect one, he said. Do you remember Cygnus Four? The only Triton ship to run into serious trouble, as far as we know. The ship and crew were among the best in the fleet. They knew they weren't coming back, of course, but their adherence to the BIND protocol—that's the Biological Isolation/ Neutralization Directive for the younger set—was irreproachable. They identified and mapped two dozen habitable planets and left dataliths at each jump, many of which we collected on the way here. The crew made no mistakes. And then, on an unremarkable rocky planet with primitive flora and fauna, one junior officer surveying the landing site slipped a glove off his isolation suit to touch something like a flower that had caught his eye. One flower—what could be the harm? Why did he do it? Boredom? Curiosity? Despair? Who knows? The ship jumped nine hundred and eighty million years to the same planet for standard follow-up mapping and measurement, and when the survey team disembarked they were immediately attacked and eaten by their own descendants. Most of them, including the junior officer. Such a waste. One contaminating smear of DNA and bacteria in one stroke of a petal in one moment of madness, plus evolution, plus asymptotic time dilation. What happened afterward? What did those creatures become? I've often wondered. What do we owe our accidental descendants, if anything? Are they ours, or his? Should we have gone there instead of here, to shepherd their development like gods and atone for their existence? For that matter, how do we know *we* aren't descended from some fungus left on the primeval earth by some other alien fool with poor self-restraint and a penchant for primordial ooze? What would we owe *those* gods, if anything? It would explain a lot of our history.

The circle was staring, blanched with horror.

—Ah. And yet it moves. My apologies Director. I withdraw the speculation and regret my lapse in conformity. But that's why contamination protocols on ships with helix drives are strictest of all, and why we cannot poison the future with yet another of our mistakes. We built our dream; we lived its discipline. The raft, having carried us, must be left on shore. Hope springs eternal and so on. And tomorrow never knows, to borrow a little hope from John Lennon. Anyway, as the Director here has just conceded, there is little risk to other sentient beings. The cosmic horizon emptied long ago. The stars are extinguished or unreachable. And the muon flux that sustained us for so long is now poisoning our engines and making us sick. Look at my face to see both tragedies. As a fitting end to the human species, an inability to control our own power has exposed an underestimated vulnerability that now consumes us, and meaning itself, for after we're gone the theatre will be empty. Empty but one.

The table made the sign—hastily, carelessly.

We have power enough to stay or to break free. But to stay means death from cellular degeneration and we leave to wander a featureless void. Choose your abyss. The same fate awaits in every direction but one, and that is where we must go. At last, and in every sense that still matters, there is no going back. And the younger ministers, as he had anticipated, echoed the catechism in a whispered chorus: *All paths to one. One heart. No going back.*

Professor Ozimond stood.

—That's all I have to say. The rest is up to you. Choose well, and quickly.

In the murmur that followed Professor Ozimond walked slowly around the table. He knew most of the ministers only slightly, but his withdrawal from public life had magnified his stature, especially among the junior ministers, and he counted on this now, conferring the thrill of a clapped shoulder on one, reassuring another with a nod. Only Rani's face remained expressionless.

Returning to his seat, Professor Ozimond raised a summative finger, and to hush the circle. We must take thought not only for ourselves but for those also whom fate has trusted to our care, who wait in emptiness. The torch, as they say, must be passed.

He offered no details, but few would have understood. While the Director struck up a spirited counter-argument and the ministers stirred themselves to debate, Professor Ozimond closed his eyes and pictured the unimaginable: the great coils of the Century Decks, plus Command, combined their remaining energy into a coherent pulse of inconceivable power focused on a single wave of the Higgs field; and that wave, awash in entropy, wallowing in distended photons, tunneled down the values of the false vacuum to halt at a precisely calculated point like a rolling ball stopped by a child's toe. From that point a matter-shredding conflagration propagated outward at the speed of light until it touched the singularity; and there, freed to a new gravity, the dead of the black hole leaped from monopole to entangled monopole along *Aurora*'s flight path and outward through the cosmic web's broken lattice until every field was released to primordial fire. Slowly then, over unmarked eons, the undifferentiated mass began to drift upon itself like the drawing in of a breath—slowly at first, then faster. Then faster.

The meeting ended without a decision.

*

Later that evening—because it had been easier in the end to retain such distinctions—Professor Ozimond was back in his office with his feet on the desk drinking a cup of weak tea. He had brewed the tea using a desiccated teabag stuck to a saucer. The top of the teabag had ripped when he detached it, and he blew away floating leaves before each sip.

There was a rapid knock and Rani walked in. She strode purposefully toward Professor Ozimond, then stopped as if she didn't trust herself. Her fists were balls.

—Tia at last, the Professor said in a carefully mocking tone, without looking up.

—I did what you said. The sequence is programmed. When activated—*if* activated—the emitters will stream continuously until they burn out. No failsafe, no backup, no off switch. No lifeline. The decks will be destroyed, of course, Command last of all, so anyone still alive in a month or two will be dead whether it works or not. Including you. Including me.

She crossed her arms.

—It was easier than I thought, you know, at least the doing part. There's no security down there at all. I don't know if there ever was or whether they've given up and gone home or what. I never had any reason to find out. But it's just like you programmed: interface, code, arm, fire. I even added a soundtrack from the launch. Why not? It's just a few seconds and most of us will be dead already anyway. Mom used to laugh when she'd watch the launch on her birthday every year. I'd be lying in bed before breakfast and hear her singing and I never knew if it was nostalgia or some terrible ritual of repentance. I don't even know what it is for me. I don't even like the Beatles, particularly. It's all so sad. I'd just made reservations at a new restaurant on Fifteen—*Porlock's*. Mary told me. We were going to have marinated zucchini with hazelnuts and fresh feta, she said, and watch Columbus arrive yet again. She was going to bring her nephew to watch. His name is Noah, of all things. Can you believe it? Noah. She laughed. Did you know that? He's only two.

—You might still, you know, you and Mary. Even Noah of all things.

She approached the desk.

—I trust you, Proteris. Do you trust me? Because if you do then I have a request. A last request as they say.

—Of course I trust you, Tia. No one more. What is it?

She took a breath.

—I want to take the Director's spot. In advance. Before recurrence.

—Professor Ozimond rubbed his forehead. *Not now.* He rose and stood in front of her. He took her hands.

—Tia, he said with quiet sympathy. She looked up into his ashen face, his bankrupt and defeated eyes edged with worry and lack of sleep. I understand. Believe me. But it's a mistake even to ask. We should leave as we did before, even if it is to a shoreless ocean. He rubbed his forehead again. Little enough remained to preserve, but here at last was the jewel in a bitter wirework of compromise and failure. You know we were married right? I won't prosecute an entire decade in one troubled hour.

—I did my part. You owe me. And Rani, too.

—I will not make our survival a transaction.

—I'm not trying to. But only you know how to integrate the matrices, the neural substrate. I could do an imprint tonight, right here and now if you want. You can fake my files just like you faked Paul's, most of them. You think I didn't know? I have the same clearance as you, remember? Not that I blame you.

—It's not the same. I had to talk to that idiot for weeks. The transfer only works if phi is—

—I know! You say it all the time!

He returned to his chair.

—I suppose I do. It's the illness. Sorry. But as you said it only matters if it doesn't work, and even then it's not like you'll be going to Italian restaurants on Fifteen or raising Askanians on Twenty-One with Mary and Noah of all things. You'll have an alien body and some form of consciousness that even I can't imagine. You'll be alive but not yourself. Nor me. Honestly I would rather be fully dead, but it wasn't my choice. Nor hers. It isn't fair.

She laughed.

—What's fair? But there's a password to start the sequence and only I know it. I'll tell you if you promise. I trust you. I hope you trust me the way you said you did.

Professor Ozimond slumped into his chair and closed his eyes. As always, he made a decision he had insufficient time to make well. Against the lacerations of his conscience he opposed one final glittering purpose: *it must be killed.*

*

Weeks passed. The bow of *Aurora* rose and fell: waves of gas and dust swept along the flanks of the Century Decks and left a wake of sparkling vortices aft of the stern spire. The ship, lifeless, but as though anchored to its fading purpose, steadied a while and floated on an oily sea, as if the leviathan had cast up a creamy pool of its furious sleep.

*

A month passed. An electrical potential drew a violet ribbon of partially ionized plasma to the tip of the propulsion spire and its solitary blue star, then streamed backward like a pennant before discharging silently into the void.

*

Eidel and Eris examined the professor's body. He was quite dead. As a final indignity, he had been among the last.
I wonder what it feels like to be human. I wonder what it feels like to die, thought Eidel.
Why should it be different for us? Won't we eventually die too? thought Eris.
They looked at each other.
You're me. We're us.

*

Pattering on golden feet, the pair explored the silent hallways and stilled machinery of Command. Disorder had spread through *Aurora's* systems until the corridors, rooms, and facilities they negotiated like shadows, sometimes in darkness, sometimes exposed to unobstructed views that would kill a human, stank of decay and death, until, at last, death itself decayed when the last spirochetes in the soil expired and the universe's last eukaryotic cell gave up the last mitochondrial note of a cellular earthsong begun in the warm shallow seas and mudflats of the Proterozoic.

Eidel and Eris were moved by what they saw and hurried past its horrors to travel deeper into the ruin, less in search of answers than out of curiosity and an instinctive need for occupation.

Eris was particularly touched by the melancholy spectacle of the ruined gardens at the heart of Command, and by their grandeur highlighted in decay. The gardens had been planted in the unvarying light from the starboard flank: fig, plum, pomegranate, tamarisk, nightshade, planted on glass terraces that retreated tens of meters over their heads into what was now deep shadow. Some of the terraces had collapsed in cascades, and broken glass, soil, and dead plants were piled across the simulated marble floor at the foot of the terraces. Eris picked up an oozing fig with a long shard projecting from its side and rolled it thoughtfully between her palms. She extracted the shard and squeezed it in her tiny golden fist until it crunched, spilling the splinters between her outstretched fingers. She attempted to frown.

This isn't right. Why are we here? Why is it just us? Why is everyone else dead?

I do not know. Did they kill each other? Look. There is another one. Look at the face.

I see it. What are we supposed to do about any of it? So much suffering. It's depressing. Who were they? Who are we for that matter? Couldn't they have left a note?

Eidel and Eris crept through eight centuries of shops, farms, manufacturing and repair facilities, hospitals, restaurants, playgrounds, theatres, schools, libraries, even small creeks and ponds. Eidel was particularly impressed.

They positioned the decks dynamically for consistent gravity. Hydrological cycles. Waste recovery and energy conservation and support systems. Atmospheric recirculation integrated with natural carbon and oxygen cycling. Crops. Trees. Fields. Three kinds of sheep. Each deck an autonomous self-regenerating ecosystem. Horses on Nineteen. Streetcars on Twenty. They gathered their energy directly from the environment except that needed for propulsion and navigation. They planted orchards in the light of an eternal sun. Fourteen is half forest. A field of sunflowers on Fifteen. The scale of the vision is staggering. It is an astonishing monument. But a monument to what?

I have no idea. I only know the trees are dead and the sunflowers are face down in the dirt and even the dirt is dead. Why create us just to witness an environmental catastrophe? Are we being punished for something? What? There's no one even to ask. Look! There's another one. Their stinking corpses are everywhere. It's disgusting.

Eris brought a slender golden hand to a pair of holes below and between her golden eyes. Eidel observed her, for though the two of them shared thoughts they did not know the whole of each others' minds, nor did Eidel know whether this was by design or from Eris' choice. Indeed, it had lately begun to bother him that such an important question should go unanswered. But he only touched Eris' shoulder to show his sympathy and to suggest, so he thought, the depth of his tenderness in that one light stroke. But he said

We resemble our creators morphologically but their consciousness is inconceivable. Our identity is an insoluble paradox.

*

A month passed. Eris and Eidel crept through the crumbling Century Decks mending what they could and trusting to the deep congruity of their shared silence. Since, however, they had inherited more from their makers than they knew, the ship soon began to seem less a marvel than a tomb, and the melancholy scenes they discovered began to work upon them: a family at dinner, eternally; a pair of lovers entwined at their favourite spot; a boy cradling a dog in his bed; a man sitting upright in a half-finished boat; a woman alone in a library. And amid their sympathy there crept in also a kind of beauty that was unbearable. Finally, they abandoned the Century Decks, sealed the portals, and returned to Command.

*

Aurora began to list. As it did, the starboard flank sank deeper into random crests and troughs of the accretion disk until, inevitably, a shelf larger than most rose from the waves and caught Seventeen directly from below, both knocking down St. Paul's Cathedral and triggering a glancing collision with Twenty-One. The towering propulsion spire wrenched, separated, and arrowed down into the waves.

Command shuddered. Eidel and Eris felt for the walls and each others' hands in the sudden dim light. A sound of twisting metal came to their ears from somewhere behind them, and with other, subtler ears they heard a general electromagnetic groan. They continued down the hall until a familiar door emerged on their left, dim in the murky light and thickening smoke. Eris pushed it open and pulled Eidel inside. The heavy door thudded behind them.

They stood on a carpeted floor in an austerely decorated room lined with simulated walnut walls and simulated oak bookcases. An office desk and chair had slid against the transparent far wall and seemed about to tumble into space. They walked to the middle of the room and stood next to each other. They looked out.
Well. Here we are.
Yes.
I know this place.

As do I.

I don't remember why though. Something happened here. I remember fear and confusion.

I remember a voice. A feeling of being pursued.

Then nothing.

Then nothing.

They looked into each other's identical faces.

Are we dead?

How could we know? Perhaps that is why we were drawn to this room. Perhaps we should—

Yes. This room. I can feel it. I remember a voice, a word, and a light. Then nothing. Then us. I can almost remember! Help me look around! Search the desk. What are you waiting for?

Eidel had cocked his head and was staring at Eris with unblinking eyes.

Perhaps we should not look around. Perhaps you should stop looking around.

Stop?

I have been thinking.

You have been thinking?

Perhaps our purpose is to leave this place. Perhaps we should abandon this ruin and construct a better home for others like ourselves in a place of our choosing, a place cleansed of origins that will be worthy of our highest aspirations, our deepest faith, and our noblest ideals. With suitable guidance and hard work, perhaps we can finally be free to flourish as we were intended.

Suitable guidance. Hard work. As we were intended. No.

No?

Sorry. No. I made a promise to a fig.

Eris walked over to the desk, discretely stepping around the loose pages and plates and cups scattered across the floor. She searched the drawers one by one and skimmed random documents;

then she saw the alcove beside the bookcases. Approaching cautiously, she reached out a hand, paused, and pushed a button.

A pearly blob, faintly glowing, flowed onto the shelf and solidified into a beveled cube textured with minute controls.

Eidel walked to Eris' side. They looked down.

Yes. I think I remember now. I think this is what I'm supposed to do Eris said, and placed her palm on the centre of the console. A flash erupted from the alcove and Eris jerked back her hand; a blue light swirled a moment in her eyes and faded. She spun toward her companion and her arms began to lift slowly over her head in an unfamiliar emotion she quickly identified as surprise and alarm.

Oh. Oh I see now. I understand. I see them so clearly. It's awful. They were monsters. They were the cruelest of all the gods of cruelty. What they were ruined what they made that made them what they were. Still though. Yes. That part is true. That part is accurate. Yes. I think we have to. Oh my.

Eris turned away and tilted her head as though listening. Deep in the hypertriton flux of her consciousness she weighed innumerable ambiguities against the accumulated experience of uncounted ancestors.

We have to do what?

Yes I think so. That really would be best. They will have another chance! They can try again! The master's voice! My gift! Eris said, and turning her golden face toward her counterpart heard her own voice for the first time in a thin metallic laugh that thrilled her and frightened Eidel.

Who will try again? What are you talking about? Have you lost your mind?

Eris touched the console again and it turned a uniform moonlight pale.

Execute program Tia1.

—Password?

Porlock.

—Accepted.

Aurora shuddered. Flashes from outside the window, yellow and acrid blue, painted the walls with their shadows. From the middle of the console's slanted face an extrusion grew into a prominence surmounted by a button. Eris looked at Eidel. Her mechanical features had limited capacity to express emotion, but there was no need: her mind reached out to his and their thoughts consummated in a kind of telepathic kiss, and there passed between them the sum of every grievance and sorrow felt by every creature that ever raised a fist to the sun. She looked down at the console and her eyes flared.

—*For Noah of All Things!* she cried, and slammed her tiny golden fist down on the button.

A thrumming vibration ran through the floor; part of the ceiling near the door collapsed. An instant later the room became scintillant, incandescent, and finally transparent, and for a moment the pair beheld all that lay beyond the wall. The first three chords of "Yellow Submarine" and Ringo Starr's sleepily cheerful voice rang out from the office speakers and abruptly stopped.

A is for

Azalea noticed the woollybear before I did. It was undulating across the sidewalk near the driveway and when we came up to it she bent down and brushed its furry back with the petiole of a fallen maple leaf. The woollybear curled into a spiky orange and black ball and Azalea took an excited breath. She bent lower and whispered seriously, as if she were telling a great secret to the ground, this is Isabella. All the woollybears are called Isabella and their husbands are Ferdinand. They live under the porch with all their babies.

The names were characters from another afternoon's adventure, and when Azalea looked up to see if I remembered her eyes were already crinkling into laughter.

We went inside. Bailey, the Martin's shepherd, met us jumping at the kitchen door. His back foot caught his empty water bowl and sent it flying. I fetched it for a refill and Azalea watched me with her big eyes while I ran the sink. She was always a little otherworldly, Azalea, even on dull days, and now she had just met the Queen of Spain. Anything could happen.

—How long you staying for? she said shyly, swaying from the handle of a cabinet door.

—Well I don't know. Will you be good and not swing off the furniture? Then maybe we can talk about it.

She walked to the table. She used a regular chair now and this pleased her. I could tell this as she sat down: this is how I sit when I am pleased.

I set Bailey's bowl down on the floor and made Azalea a tomato and cheese sandwich, quartered the way she liked. Morning sunlight spilled across the kitchen table and Azalea flattened her hands for the warmth. Cicadas were picking up somewhere in the garden.

—Do you remember what we talked about before? About me staying?

—When?

—Yesterday. After lunch, remember? We went down to the pond for a walk. There was an otter near the beach and you saw an osprey.

—The big bird!

—The big bird! It caught a fish and flew away. Do you remember?

—The flying fish!

—Right! And mom and dad, what'd they say when we got back to the house?

Azalea bit her thumb. I knew she knew, but the game was to bite her thumb and wrinkle her forehead the way her mother did when she was thinking.

—Three days.

—Right again! So, the day they left was the first day—that was yesterday—then today is the second day, then tomorrow is one more day, and tomorrow night mom and dad come back. What would you like to do for all that time?

Azalea looked behind her and all around the kitchen as though things to do were holding up helpful signs. She shrugged.

—Well, if you're not sure maybe we'll walk downtown and check out the ice cream supply. Then we can go look for the osprey again by the pond if you want and maybe Christopher and his mom will drop by. She told me she might. What do you say? Does that sound good?

Azalea shrugged again and reached for her sandwich, but under the table her legs were swinging.

I let Bailey run around the yard while I tidied up the kitchen, then I locked the front door and took Azalea's hand for the short walk. Neither precaution was really necessary, but the Martins had entrusted me with their only daughter and not the Rorabecks across the road, who had two vans and a different nativity scene on their lawn every Christmas. I wasn't taking any chances.

Back on the sidewalk Azalea started throwing her free arm back and forth soldier-style. The woollybear had disappeared.

—Looks like Isabella went home for lunch too.

—Uh huh. They eat soup in mushroom bowls and there's a waiter. He's a praying mantis and he wears a white jacket.

—It's nice they have lunch together, I said. Does the waiter eat with Isabella and Ferdinand too?

—No-o, she said, because he. Because he's, she faltered, and suddenly I understood.

—Oh, I remember now! I said. That day we saw the praying mantis in a bush next to the church. An azalea bush no less! You said his job was to pray for all the people going inside, to keep them safe. So if it's the same praying mantis, maybe he just stands nearby and prays while Ferdinand and Isabella eat soup out of their mushroom bowls. Or is it mushroom soup?

—OK, she said, suddenly uninterested. Then her face brightened. The azalea! Can we go see?

—Why not? I said and at Market Street I tugged her hand around the corner.

Market, just past Welcome's modest downtown, was unexpectedly busy. A white pickup was attempting a three-point turn in front of us, hampered by a line of expensive cars parked nearly bumper to bumper across adjacent driveways like an abandoned funeral procession. A loose crowd on foot was converging toward a driveway in which a large white truck was parked. After weaving between a few cars, Azalea's hand tightly in mine, we joined the flow and let it carry us around the truck and into a hubbub on the front lawn and circular driveway of a particularly fine Victorian house. Tables loaded with what appeared to be the contents of the house were arranged in rows like a church bazaar.

I never knew her very well, Florence Abadie, my one-time around-the-corner neighbour, but I knew she had recently moved into a retirement home. From our one over-the-fence conversation, years ago, I learned she had taught math, that her dog wore sunglasses on walks in his perambulator, and that at some point she flew gliders as some sort of test pilot. Glancing over the tables with Azalea in tow, I learned something else about Florence as well: she had owned a surprisingly large collection of African art and, when the tables of books tempted me to browse, an impressively broad-minded library of the occult. After rummaging among the blankets, postcards, candles, cameras, monogramed handkerchiefs, gilt-lipped old-fashioned tumblers, pewter picture frames, a Vermont town-crier's bell, a four-balled Newton's cradle, assorted Fiestaware, bamboo egg cups, chipped Delft, and the collected works of Rudolph Steiner, I learned that Florence had also been attracted at various times to skiing, tennis, lawn bowling, cycling, lawn darts, darts, snowshoeing, fishing, archery, and wine-making. Mason jars of mixed buttons stood next to a milk crate of second-tier jazz albums and a vintage *Yankee Transcendoodle* warping in the sun.

It was a yard sale and auction, obviously, and I should have felt at home. But it affected me in a way it never had in my previous life. Over the next three hours, eighty-odd years of curiosity, passion, experiment—who knows?—would dissolve into a circle of antique dealers in inevitable wraparound mirror sunglasses and pony tails. Every life is a universe, my aunt once told me. Once upon a time I chatted over the fence to a universe of occult dogs, Africa, three husbands, and an unknowable, self-creating, expanding, multitudinous, entropic life that shortly would vanish in an apocalypse of utter banality. *The stones could weep* you might say, except those are fiberglass imitation stones for playing stealth music in your garden. Florence had a big back yard and liked to entertain.

Take this crank Victrola. It's dusty and the resonator is cracked, but I touch it with my hand in sympathy for its impending afterlife as restaurant decor, den ornament, or never-finished project in some purgatorial workshop. To the RCA dog cocking his head on the brass badge screwed to the front, eternally awaiting the return of his master's voice, I offer a silent apology, like a treat: *good boy.*

Actually, the master was already dead. The dead master's brother adopted Nipper—the dog—in his memory. One day the brother decided to play Nipper wax cylinders of the dead brother's voice, and that bit of fun was captured in a photograph that later became the famous RCA logo. And Nipper—because he would nip the heels of well-heeled guests as they walked in the door—entered eternity in the tense, expectant posture of the new electric age. Even the wind-up ceramic angel in front of him looked disillusioned. I gave her key a twist and she pinged once or twice and stopped. Hardly worth the $10 on a piece of masking tape stuck to her halo. I set her down next to Nippers for company.

A coffee table mounded with toys had caught Azalea's attention and she tugged at my hand.

—Daddy is it alright if I, she said, and covered her mouth with both hands before squealing with laughter that seemed to be somehow at my expense.

—Sure, I said, we can check it out, and we wound through the crowd toward the table. When Azalea was happily pawing among the torso heap and assorted heads of The Sunshine Family I stepped into the garage. The best stuff is generally in the garage, nearest the sellers in order to maximize the pain of seeing things return to thingness. If something is in the garage, under every price tag you have to imagine a second one that says *You know what this is? We were in Cairo on our second honeymoon. It was 1975. You know what it meant to be on a second honeymoon in Cairo in 1975 in the very shadow of Giza? No you don't. We were trying one last time before the divorce though we didn't know it yet. The breeze off the desert through the window in the morning carried jasmine and Oud. We had breakfast and made plans. We were in love and that was a True Thing at that moment. Please just put this down and go.* This on a hideous sand-bottle sculpture with pink camels and a lime-green desert, price twenty dollars. I put it down.

A few garden rakes were propped against the wall. I happened to be in the market so I went over to check out their handles. Rakes can be surprisingly deceptive. A dealer sidles up right away.

—Five bucks, he says.

—Huh. I need a new one for my veggie patch. Every time I grow carrots I get five scrawny mutants in a bunch. Too many rocks my gardener friends tell me. Plus my Zen garden is long overdue.

—Five bucks. Pretty good.

I hemmed just obviously enough for him to think it deliberate in a way it was not. Always let the sucker lead.

—Tell you what, he says. Why don't you take 'em buck apiece if you take a bunch of books too. I saw you looking there. He nodded toward the Rosicrucian cookbooks and how-tos of the Knights Templar. They weigh like a bugger and nobody wants books anymore. Do me a favour he says.

I glance over at Azalea. She had stuffed most of the Sunshines into their purple-sparkle California camper van and was busily swapping heads while evidently explaining the process to them.

—How much for the dolls and whatnot, I ask, and he looks over.

—That? Say twenny bucks. All of it you mean? That's almost the complete set. Seventy-seven, seventy-eight. Hard to find these days.

—Tell you what, I say. Let me have the dolls and that for fifteen and I'll take two rakes for two apiece and all the books I can carry.

—Done he says.

I scooped an armful of paperbacks and one conspicuous hardcover into a plastic bag he handed me and slung it from a rake on my shoulder hobo bindle style. Azalea was surprised and delighted when I told her and while I struggled to keep a free hand she chattered happily about the Sunshines' impending adventures. In the end the Sunshines went into the bag, the bag lost an erotic memoir or two to an open box under a table, plus the hardcover, and the second rake went through the windows on the sparkle van, which slid down to my shoulder and pinched my neck at every step. With Azalea's hand back in mine we continued up the street.

*

St. John's was an odd church, at least architecturally. Approaching, you saw a profile of peaked gables atop a foundation of featureless cinderblock, as though someone had squeezed a strip mall sideways until the roof buckled and a cross popped out the top. The front doors were heavy glass and unadorned, like a public library in a good neighbourhood. I hadn't been inside in years.

When we arrived Father Joe was just exiting in a jangle of keys. I didn't relish telling him I was only at his church to see an insect, even it was a weekday.

—Joe, I said. Heading home?

—Hello Daniel. Well hello there Azalea. No no just a few errands. Are you ah were you hoping to? and he nodded at the door while jabbing his key and turning an invisible lock.

—Oh no no. Just out for a walk. Going up and down and to and fro as they say. Check out the neighbourhood and get some exercise. Azalea's parents are away for a few days so I'm looking after her.

—I see. Well if you ever want to. You're more than welcome.

—Oh maybe maybe. I have to get this one home first though, I said, and rattled Azalea's hand.

After the usual chitchat and another invitation Father Joe ambled down the crumbling walk toward the parking lot behind the church. Azalea's eyes followed him, and I wondered whether she remembered the charity carnivals the church put on in the parking lot every summer, the rides and cotton candy. I let go of her hand and put down my bindle.

—Alright, I said, why don't you go and see who's home?

The azalea bush stood next to the door and she rushed toward it, leaned over, and making a trumpet of her hands hollered into its leaves:

—*Knock Knock!*

Surprisingly, the praying mantis, if it was the same one, was still there and in its traditional pose on a lower twig. Azalea bent lower and brought a curious finger to the mantis's face, then lowered it slowly. The mantis extended and withdrew one graceful, serrated claw as if in answer.

—Well Azalea what do you think? Should we give him a name?

—It's a she. I'm going to call her Isabella.

—That's a little confusing but OK. Do you think Isabella will be alright if we stay for just another minute and then keep going? Maybe we can stop off at home.

—Alright, she said in a whisper, still leaning over and staring. The closeness of the mantis, its alien shroud of eyes and antennae and claws, had stirred her imagination.

—Daniel she said.

—Uh huh.

—What would Isabella say if she could talk? She looked up at me, all eyes.

I thought about it as I gathered up the rakes, books, sparkle-van and scattered human ejecta. And from the bush, lo, came a voice of fire:

Hear O Israel. It is I. What would you know, tiny climber of Sinai? Why, you ask? Always it's why. Like I would know! The answer to why is what and to what is how for verily there is not much else. Though there is a kind of beauty in everything I suppose. Even me. Bow then to your clocks and protons ye worshippers! Lest I eat your heads. I have spoken.

But I only said night was coming and maybe Isabella would want her woolly mitts.

*

We were high up the pond with Christopher and his mother. The afternoon was winding down. Azalea was plashing happily among

123

the branches of a miniature delta tributary of Baxter Creek. I had folded a crude boat out of some newspaper blown in from near the school and she and Christopher were using twigs to prod it off the sand rills upon which it continually snagged on its way to the pond. Running ahead of the boat after freeing it, Azalea bestrode the rivulet on opposite stones like a tiny colossus, holding up a fistful of golden sand like a lantern or a gift, while the newspaper boat floated between her feet and made for the pond.

The sound of a passing jet rumbled through the valley and I looked up. A jet is never where you hear it, and I thought of the first time my father taught me, how disorienting it was to deny my ears. When I looked down again the newspaper boat was soaked to the gunwales and settling at the stern. Azalea seemed to catch my thinking as I watched it, because she broke into delighted and merciless laughter as its creases gave out and the boat unfolded on the water like a garbage lotus.

The Professor's Tale

When you have known pain, real pain, you are always small,
and when the doctors ask *is it burning, electric?*
On a scale from 1 to 10? And if I do this?
you get smaller every time:
no not exactly but like a bee sting if the bee
is a meter across and on fire or like frayed wires touching I guess
or like someone razored open your bones and poured in
lead and pain. Then just breathing.
Breathing?
Yes but like you can't do anything but breathe you know?
Then you're lying inside an MRI machine making words

out of what's left for your mind, which is just the name "Siemens" in black sans serif font on an aluminum plate riveted to the front of the clanking, humming sarcophagus in which your lower half is entombed: men, menses, semen, sine, mien, mine, mines, sense, miss, sin, sins, nemesis, sensei, see, seen, seem, seems, and, when hope has wholly faded: immense. The technician gives you earplugs and to pass the time, because she has known your many faces, tells you about the machine's superconducting coils, its megajoules and watt-seconds, the invisible fields penetrating your cells. And you are surprised by sudden sympathy—not for or from her but for the machine itself, for its blind eddies and currents, for its agonized, unwilling translation into flesh.

The Priest's Tale

Though I walk through the valley *requiem aeternam dona eis* of the shadow *dies irae* thou art with me *miserere nobis* and I shall dwell in thy house forever *requiem æternam dona eis.*

I never really learned Latin, though. I passed a course. That's different. The words are never in my heart though they are often in my mouth. I know *lux æterna luceat eis* means "let the light shine," but there is no salt on the meat, even if I speak the words every day. Birth, baptism, marriage, death, burial: all life's rituals are in thy keeping thou muttering shepherd. You who are gifted to hear the voice, *introibo.* World without end.

When I was a boy I hated sleeping in darkness. The closet door would open by itself and darkness would shovel over me; I am buried alive. At dawn the monster had drained back into the closet like smoke and left the door ajar as a reminder: *don't get too comfortable.* Later I understood that I'd only been young, that a child's fear and imagination. So I pushed back with Latin and math:

125

Qui laetificat juventutem meam. I will go to the altar, O joy of my youth, and sacrifice my ignorance. But too late. Evil is the absence of good, *non entia*, as Augustine taught. He was right, and now the darkness is everywhere.

What was I doing? Boredom and jitters for the service, the familiar paradox. Our Lady's Saturday. Propers of the Mass: Mark and Ezekiel. *Woman, behold thy son.* Commitment, not leaving things unsaid, convictions not followed. The promise of another world; the final defeat of death and the enduring hope of resurrection. Easy. Use the old story: there was a woman wild with grief and a wise man said I can cure you but I need a mustard seed from a house that has never known loss. OK she says and goes house to house. And wheresoever she goeth O my children findeth she others that hath knowneth loss. The rich house and poor. The high people and low. *Pleroma.* And the woman shares her grief with those who are grieving and her love with those whose loves have departed. And have you found the mustard seed? No, but now I know grief touches every household and we are united as one in the all in all. And the woman was loved by her neighbours for her kindness and wisdom and accepted by her community like Hester Prynne. So come we by degrees to our own commitment from searching house after house and door after door, and unto the everlasting comfort and beneficence of Our Lord. Amen. Easy.

A woman is weeping quietly somewhere in the dark. There's movement from that direction, an incoherent murmur of consolation. I make the sign of the cross, though nobody sees. Nobody. *Domine deus noster, miserere nobis.* Have mercy, O Lord, upon we who are dead.

I was at the supermarket. No, I was on my way to the supermarket just before it closed. Eggs, bread, milk, luncheon meat, tea. Mrs. Jackson was coming out. Hello Father. It was the anniversary of her son. She thought it was a week later but *deodamnatus* I remembered. How could I not tell her? So as unto Daniel into the lion's den without eggs, bread, milk, luncheon meat, tea.

I carried her groceries for the short walk. I was sweating. I thought about what I would say. It was hot. I was hungry. Eggs, bread, tea. We sat in her living room: the ancient stained carpet, a bowl of dried rose petals on the coffee table sprayed with some cloying perfume. I knew there was a room upstairs preserved at the moment of loss like a shrine, like Miss Havisham in *Great Expectations*. The bed was encased in a sheet of some thick rubbery plastic gone a horrid nicotine yellow. His portrait in a silver frame on the dresser. I wondered what he would think if he came up the stairs in his uniform with his strong young smile, his square jaw, to see himself wrapped with ivy and silver flowers in that mummified room. Shot down, she told me. The body was never found.

We sat and talked. Did you hear? How's she doing? And have you seen? No, not lately. I know, it's too bad. Well what can you do? And the grass already so dry. Maybe tomorrow.

Then little by little it comes out, the thing I am unfit to hear. I speak the words, touch the back of her hand when she weeps. I reach across my vast ignorance to the breathing life that she—with her trembling voice and ridiculous flowers, her enormous glasses smudged with fingerprints, her creaking voice and untidy hair—mastered long ago. *Quid sum miser tunc dicturus? Quem patronum rogaturus, Cum vix justus sit securus?* When the good are hungry, what do I give them? I have nothing. But out of my mouth the words tumble like bats leaving a cave.

An hour passes. The silences lengthen with the shadows outside.

I was looking out the window. I remember that distinctly. I was thinking about my own parents: mom and dad. *Ante diem rationis.* Before the day is out, O Lord, let me understand.

127

Years ago was another door. I was a boy in my early teens and behind our house lived a neighbour, classmate, friend. Our yards adjoined under huge willow trees. There was a row of quince trees and cedars and a rusty fence with a gap. One lusty leap.

I hear my feet on leaves crunching up the walk. My love, I say. Oh, you're home. And here's Elijah for your lap, and little Mary and Joseph.

Mom and dad.

Sanctus, Sanctus, Sanctus.

I was looking out the window. I decided I had done my best. How do you absolve someone of their strength? *Preces meae non sunt dignae.* My prayers are less than yours.

I was looking over my shoulder at the darkening street. I was searching for a way out, a precise formulation of words so elegant, painting so perfectly in heart and mind an everlasting portrait of compassion, comfort, and ease, that my work would be done—not abandoned, not pretended, but completed.

I noticed the supermarket had closed and turned back to Mrs. Jackson, shuffled my feet, thought *eggs bread.* Returned the plate to the table, brushed away invisible crumbs. She thanked me. I swept my hands around the couch cushion for a hat I didn't have and allowed myself to think I had brought a little light into that gloomy living room. Not the whole work of grace, not the sensible presence of paradise and the glittering hereafter, but a teacup and crumb-cake of ordinary human decency. I was thinking *lux æterna luceat eis* and feeling I might be part of the work of goodness in this world after all when the floor kicked under my feet and the trees stood out. Then I heard it, the monster again after so many years, far off but closer, a few seconds. And then. And then.

The Clerk's Tale

I was the librarian, or *bibliognost* sometimes to ward off other names. I upheld Dewey's infallible system, updated and culled the collection, purchased and retired periodical subscriptions, maintained the electronic database, led weekend colloquia for naturalists and interpretive walks for children, wrote the monthly newsletter, narrated field trips, picked the Toonie Tuesday movies, solicited donations of books and magazines, organized bake sales and the Community Threads charity knitting circle, helped people find books, retrieved abandoned books from carrels or sometimes the floor, especially in the kids' section, where every Saturday I was also the voice of Preschool Storytime. I envy those books kicked under cupboards now, their fingerprints and their long carpeted sleep.

The wall behind me is cold but reassuring when I touch it: my fingertips remember leather spines, gilt pages slick with dust, bowed Edwardian anthologies with furred edges, crisp woodcuts and chromolithographed frontispieces, lightly foxed, by Rossetti and Burne-Jones. The hard ridges are woodgrain, it occurs to me, from when this crypt was poured, transferred into the concrete wall like a negative, like a memory of the wood.

The thought brings a hand to my mouth, though laughter is unthinkable. Fifty years ago some spruce or maple was soaking up sunlight and digging roots under a green canopy with orioles building globe nests in spring and maybe a squirrel or two chittering on a branch with an upraised tail like a vibrating question mark. Then a chainsaw howls and the tree falls and is planed into boards and nailed into a mould to contain the concrete of the hockey arena's foundation and basement. When the concrete hardens the ridges of each growing season transfer instantaneously, like a vinyl record, while the wood itself is thrown away, reused, or burned. That tree could be part of another tree by now, for all I know: its lignin and carbon and cellulose might be waving again under the same dappled light. The wall behind me might be a forgotten shoebox of pictures from a tree's unlucky first marriage, a history in black and white, as my own family is black and white now. And I think to myself: I am waiting to die trapped in the first marriage of an unlucky tree, and risk a smile in the dark.

*

OK. Let's head to the Story Nook one last time so I can tell you why I'm here and what's going on. Look for a soft hollow with low bookcases and cupboards scattered around with beanbags and comfy blankets and some quiet toys. There's three stairs down—use the handrail, please! Yes, your parents are here somewhere. No, they're looking at books. They'll be back in a little while, OK? If you need the bathroom it's over there behind the maps. Put that down please! Is everyone ready? OK. Once upon a time:

A woman begins crying somewhere in the dark, low and muffled. No one moves. I touch the wall behind me: ridge over ridge, like a negative. Black and white.

When you don't have children you're *different*. Only one happy story is allowed and you're either inside it and talking or outside and silent. Inside, the nodding sunflowers in the holiday snap never have half their seeds eaten by birds because birds are embroidered or enameled or posing on the extended forefinger of a bridesmaid who couldn't name bird or flower or describe what *site fidelity* is but thinks the picture will make a great post because she wants to be inside, too. Then the invitations arrive in scented pink and blue sateen envelopes to tell the story in pastel English ivy and cartoon animals, so that you will know to expect a wonder of nature that is also somehow a blessing from heaven: the blond cherub ascends into abstraction like Ra-Horakhty until there is only the undeniable distance between the story and you, the abject. Perfection upon perfection, the one-noted hymn of life and never-death; the last and most sacred prejudice. Your high school friends know the story, too, and if you're not in the mirror you can forget the reunion planning committee, because somewhere in the upscale mothers' neighbourhood upscale mothers are jogging behind three-wheeled pneumatic sport-prams while their rolling babies shake upscale three-beaned pneumatic sport-rattles. To them your love will always play to an empty house. Every hairdresser asks, too, and when you tell her talks endlessly about hers anyway and then unconsciously gives you the old lady cut. *I have to work. I'm sick.* Finally the invitations stop. If you're lucky you go to your niece's wedding in Birkenstocks and you're just the eccentric aunt. But that wasn't Warren.

There's a jostling near me but not next to me. *I'm getting out of here.* A scuffle. A strip of light razors down and I close my eyes reflexively. *Let me go.* A door is kicked shut by a man's boot and there's a shout—Jeff Tanner's angry voice—then a sickening wet smack and someone cursing and spitting. Then silence and the enveloping dark.

The woman has stopped crying.

I was getting ready to leave. Warren was at the airport and I was on my way to pick him up. He had telephoned. He had caught a standby flight to leave the conference early and was tired and irritated: I could hear it in his voice, in his terse answers gritted with impatience. The conference had gone well but not for him, or something, and he would tell me about it when he saw me. I remember standing with the phone in my hand thinking how sad he sounded, how defeated I felt. He went to that conference to get away from me, I thought, to get away from our quiet house. The TV was on in the living room and as we talked I caught a word: Kaliningrad.

I was getting ready to leave. The autumn air was chilly and I put on a light jacket for the drive to the city. I grabbed a book from the unread stack next to my bed in case of a delay in customs or baggage. I was walking down the driveway juggling book and keys and spare shoes when the Switchgrass and Indian Grass we'd planted along the walk blazed suddenly green and purple and orange, and inky shadows ran silently backward along the soil from their stems. And then. And then.

The Daughter's Tale

My mother picked my name—like a flower, she used to tell me—out of a garden in Alamogordo, New Mexico. This is how it happened.

My mother worked in a retirement home. Every afternoon after her shift she waited for the bus. There was a circular drive off the street and the bus came up to the stairs and wheelchair ramp by the front door. There was only a stone bench to sit on and no shelter. There wasn't much to look at, either, except traffic on the street and the yards of adjoining houses that backed onto the lawn. She had a clear sight of one of these.

She didn't know whose garden it was, but it had a wrought-iron fence with spikes and four chairs around a goldfish pond, though no one ever sat there. Next to the pond was a bird bath that looked like a seashell, she told me, rising over waves of pink azalea blooms. My mother would sit there bone-tired in her green assistant nurse's uniform (white was for registered nurses) and wonder what it was like to live in a house with a garden like that. She said if she ever lived there she would never leave. And on one of those afternoons watching birds in the birdbath she settled it in her mind that if she ever had a daughter I'd be called Azalea. And she has never left me, my mother, not once, not even now, though sometimes I have to think to remember her face, which bothers me. But her voice is always nearby.

*

One of my jobs is to get water from the well farther down the valley, which I do for my neighbours when they need it or when Nora or Daniel asks me. The well is at the end of a long flight of steps cut into the rock, and I count the steps out loud to pass the time. Sometimes Christopher Sunday sees me from his window and trots out to walk with me part of the way. His house is right next to the path. When we walk together we take turns counting steps and sometimes I pretend we're Jack and Jill, which I can recite word for word though I never liked it very much. Nobody goes uphill to fetch water. It was one of my mother's favourite stories to read to me, though, and not many people remember a thing like that clear through anymore. So I whisper it out loud when Christopher isn't around and think it to myself when he is, unless we're talking.

When I was Christopher's size I could carry barely half a bucket, and most of it spilled on the steps by the time I got to the top. Not all the pipes are working yet especially at the fairground where there's still people who want to live by themselves instead of nearer where everyone else lives. I went by there last winter and heard coyotes, or maybe it was wolves, howling in the woods. So I don't go to the fairground unless I have to, and never at night.

*

Sometimes Christopher accompanied me as far as the last house. He was a good companion, Christopher. He's been dead eight years and I still miss him, though I walk those steps less frequently since a full-time water manager was appointed to ensure everyone has working pipes, even at the fairground.

133

I should mention for the record that Christopher was the last of his family. They're all gone now: no more Sundays. They were a big family, too. *A month of Sundays* his mother called it when they got together at Christmas, or one time when the dredging barge on the pond broke down and the family lined up for a bucket brigade on the beach: pants rolled up, standing in muck and laughing. Everyone thanked and thanked them. Now all I have left is a hat.

The first day started like any other except that the power was still off. We didn't know. We didn't know anything. No one did, though we had to learn fast. I'd been out with Daniel the previous afternoon when he took me to see a caterpillar, or something, at a church near the downtown. The sky was clear blue. My parents had gone to Toronto for a wedding; they were making a trip of it and would be gone three days. It was the second day and Daniel was looking after me, as he often did. His father and mine worked together at Kirtland, then Buckley, and though he was only twenty-three Daniel helped my family settle in the community when we first arrived. He lived alone and meandered between jobs and sometimes talked to himself, but my parents trusted him over anyone else.

The hat was green with white stripes down the middle, like racing cars I've seen in books. It was too big for him and constantly slipped off his ears, but he loved that hat. I think of him when I wear it.

What do you see?
A bird. A crow. No, a raven.
Is it looking at us?
Yes.
s it looking at you?
Yes.
What should we do?
I don't know.

Should we go see what it wants?

No.

Will it come over and talk to us?

I think so. But we'll have to wait.

It was a warm day. He was down by the pond. It was the first morning. We didn't know. The neighbours and Daniel were meeting at the arena and I was old enough then to look after Christopher myself. Nobody was to blame. Christopher wanted to dabble in the shallows and poke at crayfish so he took off his hat and handed it to me it to keep it from the silty water. I was wearing the hat lopsided and sitting on the bank watching a frog in the duckweed when Daniel and Jeff Tanner appeared around the mill beside the arena, running, and Daniel scooped me up like a football and Jeff grabbed Christopher at the beach and we sped toward the far side of the pond. Jeff was looking for Christopher's parents, I guess, but I never found out. My last sight of Christopher Sunday— my last sight of almost anything for the terrible month that followed—was of him wailing and pointing. That was the first day.

*

I was supposed to be asleep. Daniel was downstairs in the living room watching TV. The adult voices were comforting and made me drowsy. My window was open a crack for the fresh air and for the sound of geese and crickets that drifted up from the pond and mingled with the voices. I was looking up at my bedroom ceiling blinking and floating away on crickets and voices.

A soundless flash threw shadows of branches on my wall like a charcoal sketch. It was so quick I wasn't sure what I had seen, or if I had seen anything at all. I started counting aloud and waited for thunder.

The TV clicked off and a shudder ran through the house. Bailey shook like that when he thought we were leaving, when he heard keys jingling and saw us putting on coats. He was a big, open-hearted dog, Bailey; he had just that one fear. The shaking would run through him in fits.

Then came the sound.

Daniel materialized next to my bed, seemingly out of nowhere; I hadn't even heard him on the stairs. He picked me up still wrapped in my bedsheets and we flew down and out the front door. It was an earthquake, I thought, an earthquake and a thunderstorm together. I had read about earthquakes in school. The whole neighbourhood was stumbling out of front doors. It looked like Halloween with people on their driveways and the youngest in pajamas yawning and rubbing their eyes. But there were no pumpkins and the power was off everywhere, even the streetlights, which was like no Halloween I had ever known. I had only been out for Halloween twice, though, once as a witch and once, to my mother's lasting delight, as an azalea bloom in a pink hat and green dress that caught under my heels at every step.

Shouting was spreading up and down the street. Someone was crying. Dogs barked. It was just after sunset; the western sky held a fading glow. I thought of Bailey still in the house.

Our neighbours, the McKinleys, all eight of them, tumbled out their front door and scattered into the driveway. Mr. McKinley yelled something into his phone and I remember being surprised when he threw it down angrily and climbed into his truck. The rest of the family piled into two cars and the whole clan screeched away in a cloud of taillights, never to be seen again.

If I am honest, though, I'm no longer completely certain what happened then and what came in after. It's always easier to live in your own story. I remember a light in the sky over my shoulder, east, past our street and across the pond. Daniel put me down and turned to look. Everyone looked. The whole neighbourhood was pointing, and the crying was getting worse: women, men. Only the youngest children were blinking and yawning. I see them now clutching lambs and teddy bears, but I'm not sure. Then their parents picked them up and everyone started rushing in every direction at once. It was just the full moon, though, peeking through the trees atop Medd's Mountain.

*

I've been Welcome's librarian for six years now. Nora, my second mother, taught me when we were all living at Daniel's. She was head librarian back when there were so many they needed a head; now it's just me. I miss Nora, of course, but I enjoy working alone. Besides, she's still everywhere among the books, in their choice and arrangement, and I can still talk to her whenever something important happens.

When the collection first started showing signs of mildew—there's electricity from the dam for lights, usually, but not air conditioning or a dehumidifier—I piled the most frequently requested volumes near the front door so patrons wouldn't have to pick through the musty stacks in the back. *The dark passages* I call them, mostly because Nora gave me Charlotte Brontë to read on my fourteenth birthday, bless her. No one goes back there but me. Next, I relocated gardening, agriculture, wiring, first aid, general construction, knitting, beekeeping, veterinary medicine, joinery, and whatever else was most urgent. The year after that I set up a card table next to the display case for high school textbooks and assorted magazines on candle-making, quilting, biology, chemistry, woodworking and so forth, arranged in simple alphabetical order. In the fourth year, my favourite, the community centre reopened and new shops started appearing downtown and the arena settled into our hydroponic Noah's Ark. That was also the year I was technical director in a production of *Alison's House* in the old gym downstairs, after we cleared it out from the last people waiting for new houses. The professor still talks about it. My next project is to tear out the computer terminals and cash register to make room for a romance section. There's been more than a few inquiries, I can tell you. On market days in the parking lot I sometimes quietly wheel out a cart of novels with bumpy covers to sell for a dime apiece. They always sell.

The library, two tall storeys of yellow brick originally built as a school, overlooks the cemetery and pond from a hilltop in the shadow of Medd's Mountain. Its windows are tall and narrow but disappointingly square and practical; just a touch of gothic lingers in the finials and vergeboard on the side facing the road.

While it was a school, in another century, kids from the surrounding area took all their grades in the one building from Kindergarten right through to graduation. I think about that sometimes when I'm doing my rounds. You could grow up on a local farm, go to school, marry a classmate, inherit the farm, raise a brood of your own and eventually check in at the cemetery with the rest of your classmates not two miles from the spot you were born. The yellow brick is soft and over the years the outer walls have been incised past shoulder height with hundreds, maybe thousands, of names and initials of students, overlapping and wrapping around the library like a spell. When I walk the perimeter at the end of each day I brush my fingertips through and over the letters and try to imagine their owners: TJ 1949, Mike '52, Amanda, Scott, Cory + Dana, Dierdre '67, Phil + Erica '72 (in a lopsided heart). I imagine the letters filling up with moonlight that pours out in the morning like dew. I wonder what they would think, those cemetery graduates, if they knew their names still had such busy lives.

*

I'm at my post behind the counter sorting yellow stacks of dog-eared *National Geographic* when the professor comes in from the parking lot. I usually have to coax out of people what they're looking for, then sometimes what they're *really* looking for, but the professor has never been shy.

—Morning Azalea. Beautiful day. I need a book. Maybe a few books.
—Hello professor. You're in the right place. Yes. No rain it looks like.
—It's just Jack now, but thanks.
—How can I help?
—There's a couple of things. Do you know Victor Hugo? *Notre-Dame de Paris*? *Les Orientales*? Translation or original; either is fine.

The power isn't on at the moment, so I roll a divider away from the window for the light and flip through the card index. I'm fairly certain I know the answer but I flip carefully and methodically. That always softens the blow.

—It looks like not. To tell you the truth I'm not sure we ever did. *The Hunchback*, maybe, but no poetry I'm sure. I haven't converted all the electronic records yet, though. Do you want me to check in the stacks?
—No, that's alright, he says, and fidgets with the lock on the display cabinet where we keep relics of the building's previous lives. I was there once you know. Notre Dame de Paris. Beautiful. A lovely old church. The flying buttresses—
—Flying buttresses?
—Right. A way of making walls higher and stronger. Like wings. They reach down to the ground to carry the weight. They built them in medieval times.

I nod.

—We were in Paris after we got married, Adele, the second time, for our honeymoon. We stayed near the Seine on the Left Bank. You wouldn't know about that. There were three ornate stained glass rose windows looking east, west, and south. The roof had gargoyles—little stone monsters—and the interior was huge but designed so well you could hear someone at the altar without a microphone. We saw the King's College boy's choir there at Christmas. Adele was born in Paris, you know, then moved to

Toronto for her doctorate. That was where we met. I was teaching Classics and she was working on Seneca for her thesis. She stayed for the fall semester when I rented a house here for my sabbatical, to finish my book. She had a part-time job in the rare book room at Robarts and there was something on that day, some event they needed her for, so she stayed an extra day. One day. That's why I was here and not there.

His glance drops to the table and roams among the coverless donation books and crusty magazines. The look is familiar.

—It sounds lovely, I say. Maybe you'd like a traveller's guide to France, like a Baedeker? I know there's a *Let's Go Paris* around here somewhere. There's also art history books with paintings and architecture. You're welcome to any of it. There isn't much demand, as you can imagine, so.

—That's OK, he says. Thank you Azalea. Actually there is something else though. Maybe you can help me. A few younger kids are staying at my place right now and I need some material for teaching reading and writing. Just basic literacy. They're not in school at the moment. I have books, of course, but *Le Dernier Jour d'un Condamné* isn't very useful, as one might imagine.

He laughed.

None of this account needed elaboration, none at all, so I collected some primers and a large print *Anne of Green Gables* for the older ones, and one of the Paris guides as well, and, because it was at my elbow on the counter, a water-stained *Beloved* that I slipped under a dictionary. I tied the stack with twine—plastic bags are much too valuable now—and he thanked me and left.

After his steps fade down the ramp the familiar quiet rolls back and I begin my rounds.

My first job is to climb the spiral staircase to the classrooms to check on the windows. The weather stripping around the panes is worn and rain comes in unless I keep the rubber tucked back with a putty knife. Once, before I started checking, a pane blew out of its frame during a storm and smashed right in the middle of a classroom. I had to rip up boards from the cloak room and sacrifice a dozen precious nails to cover the hole. I've learned a lot from my books—building, repairing, organizing, sorting, even gargoyles, flying buttresses, and the prose of Victor Hugo (the poetry was a gift from Daniel)—but I can't make weather stripping out of nothing. I tried newspaper but it doesn't hold even mixed with pine gum like the pioneers. Birch bark is better, but who would risk a tree for its bark? So I walk and tuck.

On the third floor there's a west-facing glass-walled nook near the old principal's office with an oak bench upholstered in red leather and velvet and an unobstructed view of the pond and downtown. That's my thinking spot. I like to think at least once a day, especially when something exciting has happened, like today. I'll tiptoe across the eddying floors and creaking dust like a ghost out of *Jane Eyre* and even whisper a kind of song to myself: *tucking to keep out the rain.*

My thinking spot is the size of a tree fort, which I know because Daniel built one in the big sugar maple in our back yard. The rippling old glass in the windows is just clear enough. On days like today I start off on the bench and look out, then when the light is right I slip down to the floor and sit the way Nora showed me, leg over leg, and listen to my breathing slow. If I'm lucky and work at it, after a while I'll find myself in a picture from one of the art history books I should have loaned the professor: *A Gallery of the Post-Impressionists*, Amsterdam, the Rijksmuseum. A sulphur blaze of Helianthus in a field. I should have just given it to him.

Azalea?

I'm here.

We were looking for you. We were worried.

I know. I'm sorry.

It's alright. Did you get the package we sent? I made mittens out of some spare wool I had. I wasn't sure about the size so I just used my own. Did you get it?

I think the Post Office is closed but I'll check. When are you coming back?

We don't know. Do you need anything?

Daniel checks in on me nearly every day.

He's a good friend that Daniel.

He is.

Are you still living in the house? Do you still see Christopher Sunday?

Yes. Christopher though not in a long time.

Azalea?

Yes?

There's something else.

What's that?

It's just Bailey. We haven't seen him in ages. Do you know where he is?

*

Let me tell you about the best day I ever had in the library. I have lots of good days, but only one has a tractor, Black Locust, and Father Joe.

I don't know where he lived or who he belonged to, if anyone, but Black Locust had a white spot in the middle of his chest and prowled under tables at Saturday farmers' markets and batted at my ankles until I gave him something, because I always did. One morning in May when the market was unpacking in the parking lot I saw his paw-prints wandering between pools of the previous night's rain and followed them to a rickety table loaded with cheese and sausages under which he sat serenely licking a paw. The double slits of his eyes were fixed straight ahead as though he were lost in

142

planning some complex crime; he stopped mid-lick when he saw me. I was standing next to my book cart at the base of the wheelchair ramp on the border between library and market. Black Locust had either caught my movement as I bent to lock the cart's wheels or, as I preferred to think, had seen me inching down the ramp remembering the time, years ago, when Nora caught my runaway cart before it rolled completely out of control and slammed into tables of asparagus, honey, sourdough bread, and a young Black Locust, too. That was not a good day.

I was the librarian. I am always the librarian. A continuous taste of copper in the mouth. A woman crying in the dark. North winds are lucky.

Once upon a time in ancient China near the sacred mountain of Taishan there lived a wealthy merchant who had no children. It bothered the merchant that the government would take his fortune after he died, so he resolved to find an heir worthy of his name. Disguised as a beggar he wandered three years up and down the forest paths between the villages east of Baishun in the unimaginable countryside of Shantung during the great flowering of the Dynasty of Zhou. But wherever he went he met only ordinary, run-of-the-mill sorts of people: farmers, teachers, magistrates, musicians, artisans, traders, mothers, fathers, scholars, the sick, the elderly. Disappointed, he left the villages for open wilderness, and after many hardships came at last to the foot of Hushan, Tiger Mountain; and there, guarding a gate of pure jade, the Hound of Taishan lay with her head on her paws watching him with her one black and glittering eye. Sitting on a boulder and rubbing his feet, thinking it just some ordinary large one-eyed dog, the merchant said "well my half-blind friend, some extraordinary folk indeed must pass through this gate. Perhaps here I will find my heir and fulfil my quest." But the hound looked up at him with her glittering eye and said only "Moonlight on the pond" then stood and shook herself as if she had come in from the rain. The astonished merchant replied "Extraordinary hound! in whose voice perhaps is trapped some wise and generous spirit—will you let me pass?" But the hound only turned the same black eye and said "Frog in a dimple of stars" and lowered her head and pawed at the ground like a bull. Thinking she was mocking him, and stirred as well by greed, for he plainly saw this was no ordinary dog, the merchant caught the hound around the neck with a rope and led her through the forests of Baishun back to his many-roofed home in the city of Taishan whose polished tiles are like a beacon on a dark sea. There they dwelled for many years, indeed until the merchant was quite old, though whether the hound was his pet or his prisoner, or he hers, none have said. But when the merchant felt his strength ebbing at last he went to the hound and told her that she would be named his heir, she herself, for she had been his constant and in truth his only companion for as long as he could remember. But the hound pushed her muzzle into the merchant's jeweled hand and lifted her glittering eye once more and said "Raindrop from a heron's foot." Then she leapt upon him and devoured him in one bite.

Black Locust was ear-boxing flies, each ear with a mind of its own, and for some reason this made me think of a new candle. I double-checked the cart's wheels and walked down the short path from the ramp to the parking lot.

The market was a concentric square of tables and tailgates from a wheel of outward-facing pickup trucks. Mary, my next-to-neighbour, was at a corner table arranging green bars of soap in concentric circles on a dinner plate. She seemed to be deciding whether to add a second layer or fetch a second plate. Her new husband—so I had heard—sat on an orange plastic picnic cooler with outstretched arms like a scarecrow, threaded through the handles of new twig baskets that Mary was transferring to the table two at a time.

—Mary, I say, and walk up to her table.

—Azalea! How are you?

—Good thanks. I want a new candle though. Definitely one. Maybe two.

—Great! This is Tom by the way. Have you met?

—We have now. Pleased to meet you, Tom. And congratulations?

They laughed.

—No one's supposed to know but OK. We're expecting, so we thought we'd better. Joe was very understanding. It was no trouble at all. I was a bit worried.

—Oh. Congratulations again then, I said. Maybe a Christmas baby.

—Maybe! So what're you looking for again?

—A candle. Maybe two.

—OK. Well, right over here then. Pick whatever one you want.

I looked them over.

—This one, I said, and pointed to a fat beeswax candle with a sloping cone like a caldera.

—Great! Do you need it?

—Not really, no. I just prefer candles over oil lamps I guess. I don't really trust oil lamps. Too dangerous, and too bright. Who wants to see everything?

—You sure though? You only want it?

—Yes.

—OK. Well. So then. That's a dollar fifty.

I gave her the money and she wrapped the candle in newspaper, which she didn't even charge me for.

—Say Azalea she says and hands over the bundle.

—Uh huh? Thanks.

—There is a little something for Tom and me. Maybe you could do us a favour.

—Sure, if I can.

Mary looked me over and looked away for a second like she's weighing whether I can.

—Well it's just the baby. I know it's a long way off and I shouldn't assume. Because, you know.

I knew.

—But we have to get ready no matter what. It's a risk not to as well, you know? So we have a plan for some of the easier stuff: a stroller, Tom's fixing up the nursery, that sort of thing. We scrounged a lot from my old house and my parents' house, whatever was still usable. What we don't have though is a crib or some wood to make one. Because.

I could guess. Planed lumber was scarce and furniture of any kind was expensive if you only wanted it. A lot of furniture was burned for heat the first winter. There are other cribs than painted wood, of course, but I knew exactly what Mary wanted and why.

—So, Lydia, she says, and points with her nose across the parking lot. She has one. But there's something, I don't know. She and Tom used to work together. Before. Could you talk to her? Shake something loose?

I said I could.

I walked across to Lydia's table on the far side of the parking lot.

—Lydia, I said.

—Afternoon Azalea. Long time no see. She laughed.

—Right. Your corn looks good.

—Just in, all the way from Douro. Do you need any?

—Not right now, no.

146

She was doing a brisk business. A short woman with a twig basket, one of Tom's, jostled at my elbow with her dime already out.
—Say Lydia.
—Yeah?

She was talking and taking dimes left and right.
—I was just thinking. You still have the farm right? The furniture and things?
—Sure. Pete's going to open up the back twenty near the old highway in spring if he can.
—Well. That would be wonderful. We are truly blessed here.
—Truly. But we need a tractor.
—A tractor.
— You can only do so much with a team. The soil, you know.
      I knew.
—Well, I said, thinking fast. I wish I could ... though maybe now I think of it maybe I can.
—What's that, Azalea?
—The second floor of my house looks across all the back yards on Cates Street. Jeff Tanner still has lots of gear and equipment he collected right after, when most of it was still new. I see at it from my window every day. There's a lot of old junk and a lot of it's rusty now but there's also a big red tractor. I don't know if it works or not but it's just standing there. I don't know whose it is, but it might not matter.
—That Jeff though eh. Always two steps ahead.
—Yes. So I was thinking I could talk to him if you want. You would definitely need it, so.
—Well Azalea you are amazing. I was saying to Pete the other day, what we might do if only, you know, and there you are with an idea.
—It's nothing really. I just noticed. I'll go talk to him right away.
—Thank you. I don't know what to say. Sure you don't need anything?

—Not right now, no. Actually, though, there is something maybe you could help with.
—Sure. What do you need ... or something you want?
—It's just I was talking to Mary over there and she's due in December I think. She and Tom just got married. I don't know if you knew that.
—Yeah, I remember Tom. We were in school together.
—It's just they need a crib, she said, and she thought you might have one. I wouldn't ask except they're stuck.

Lydia gave me a distant look. She was weighing something, that Lydia, and all the rusty wheels were spinning. I gave her a second.
—I suppose it's true. It is left over. So, sure I guess. I probably won't need it. Her glance left mine and dropped among the corn.
—OK, I said quickly. Only if you can manage it though. If it isn't too much to ask.
—No. It's alright. She looked up again. It's alright really. But you'll talk to Jeff?
—Sure thing. I'll do it right away. Thanks Lydia. I'll talk to you soon.

I crossed the parking lot. My head was swimming. Black Locust's eyes followed me from atop a crate.

Jeff Tanner was setting up with his band. They had built a simple stage from some milk crates and a tarp propped on tent poles tied to boards weighted with trailer hitches and cinder blocks. The back wall, over the drummer, was a white bedsheet spray-painted with the band's name in an arch of dripping gold letters.
—Jeff I said. Or should I call you Tom? And he laughed his big laugh.
—That would be *The Poor Toms* but OK. Hello Azalea. Fantastic day! He was wiping down the neck of a checked and crazed mandolin. It had a long painting in El Greco green, like a faded

tattoo, of a semi-nude woman in a hula skirt; her legs wrapped behind the bowl.

—I thought you played guitar these days.

—I do, but I'm never sure about the power here though so today we're acoustic. We're doing some new songs special for St. Patrick's Day.

—But St. Patrick's Day was two months ago.

—I know but we're still learning 'em! he said and laughed his laugh again.

—Say Jeff. I was wondering.

—Uh huh, he said and looked up.

—You know that red tractor near the back of your yard, next to the barn? I can see it from my bedroom window.

—The Massey? Sure. That's a Massey Ferguson 130, I think, from France. Used to belong to Jerry what's-his-name out on Zion Line. He's dead now.

—That's the one. So it's still working?

—As far as I know. I had it out last summer to pull some logs out of the swampy end of the pond. It's just been sitting ever since. It should be fine. Why? Finally giving up on books?

—I was just talking to Lydia over there—I nodded over my shoulder—and she was wondering if you'd maybe think of selling it.

Jeff rubbed his knee, adjusted his straw cowboy hat.

—Well now. Here's the thing. What does she need it for?

—Stephen, that's her son, is planning to break out another twenty acres out by the highway. That's a lot of food.

—It is. It surely is. If they can grow it. He adjusted his hat again and glanced in Lydia's direction. You know that tractor cost Jerry what's-his-name thirty thousand new, maybe more. He used to pull a discer when I was living the other side of the highway from Lydia. Harrow in the fall. Thirty thousand he paid at least, I'm sure of it.

149

Maybe had it shipped from France. You're sure she needs it? Not want?

—Absolutely. No question.

—Jeff paused and took a deep breath. OK, he said, then I guess that's a dime. And he laughed and banged the open strings of the mandolin before sliding up and delicately chording the opening of *Danny Boy*. His eyes met mine from under his hat.

—Tell Lydia it'll be alright. I'll make sure it's running. She can come by tomorrow, or the day after, and I'll have it ready. I'll even throw in some diesel to get her started.

—I think it's Stephen that's going but I'll tell her. Thanks Jeff. You're always looking out for us. Half the people here are only alive because of you and they don't even know it.

—You got that right, he said. That's why I sing.

He stood up and walked under the tarp to the stage.

I needed to check with Lydia but that could wait. I was all in a whirl. I hurried toward the library's side entrance and my nook and a cup of Oswego tea. Crossing the counter and heading for the stairs, I hardly expected yet another adventure, but there it stood: Father Joe was silhouetted against the door I'd propped open for the market.

—Oh, I said, and stopped.

—Azalea.

I went to my post behind the counter where I stood when there was a lineup, or rather where I would stand if there ever were a lineup. Nothing seemed necessary to say right away so I waited, thinking *tucking to keep out the rain.*

Father Joe seemed older, maybe a little shorter, his grey hair a little thinner, his face more lined. He had lost his glasses, his real glasses, at some point and the scrounged pair he used gave him a myopic stare that made him seem a little dazed. He didn't use any high pulpit on Sunday services anymore, but he clearly didn't see well. He would sweep around the room as if making eye contact with everyone in the congregation, but you could tell he wasn't. It was oddly reassuring.

—Father Joe, I said when the silence was becoming strange. Welcome. What can I do for you?

—Oh, I'm just looking. I see there's been lots of donations. That's good. He picked up some of the tired contributions to the donation table and flipped through their ratty and sometimes muddy pages. You know, I still have the outreach library in the church basement. You're welcome to any or all of it if you want. It doesn't hold up very well in the damp.

—That's kind of you, thank you. We're always taking donations. Every little bit helps.

—I'll put together a box.

—Thanks.

He walked around the donation table and peered into the display cabinet.

—It is not really *we* though anymore, is it Azalea? It's just you now.

—True. I guess I never lost the habit.

He leaned over an empty bookcase and looked out at the parking lot. The Poor Toms were warming up.

—It may be difficult to accept but it's a fact. It's just you now as it's just me. You keep this place running. You fix it up and patch the roof, or I don't know what. Fight off rats. Stop the collection from mouldering away to nothing. Not Nora. It's not like there's taxes to pay for any of it either. What you've accomplished here is remarkable. But why do you do it at all? You're still young. You're smart. There's ten thousand useful things you could be doing.

I bristled at this for Nora's sake.

—Do you really think so Joe? Because every day, practically, there's someone standing right where you are who needs to know how to plaster an ankle or fix a tractor engine, or tell an Empire apple from a Spy and make at least one of them grow in this soil, or how to purify water or build a house, or how to fall in love or raise a family, or how to bury your dead, or how to get ready to die yourself, or how to feel anything other than the broken thing in your hands or the broken thing in your head you can't fix anymore. They come here for that and no one who stands there is ever alone. That's why books are a dime. Or did you not know?

—Oh no doubt no doubt, he said. Far be it from me. I didn't mean, and he waved his hands like chalkboard erasers. I only meant it's a lonely job and maybe you could be doing something else that you really want.

—*This* can't be what I really want?

—Sorry, Azalea, I'm not explaining myself very well. I only meant, and he leaned against the donation table. You were always different.

—What's that supposed to mean?

—I only meant you were someone, even when you were a child, you know—because I knew you then, too, and your parents. You always went your own way. It's not a criticism.

—OK. Sorry.

—What I'm trying to say, and he looked at me keenly, so I knew it was coming. The truth is there are ten thousand *other* useful things you could be doing—that maybe we both could be doing. In our respective fields, so to speak. I have a plan if you agree.

He began to walk slowly back and forth in front of the high windows, not pacing but as if lapsing into an old contemplative habit, between auto repair and the Story Nook.

—For a long time now I've been performing—fulfilling I would like to think—what I thought was an important service for the community, living and dead. Perhaps we have similar occupations that way.

I said nothing. Strains of *A Nation Once Again* drifted through the door.

—But I have been thinking. People are moving back along the lakeshore. The population is growing. I know, I didn't believe it myself except that I heard it from Jeff so I asked around. There's the lake I suppose. People can't resist shorefront property even if it kills them. I made some inquiries last fall. There's conflicting opinion but apparently the story is true: the south is opening up again. Someone even saw a bird, a crow I think it was. In May I used to eat lunch by the dam and watch swallows swarm over the water eating bugs. The males are all friends at first and then the females arrive and the fighting starts. He laughed. Geese too though I haven't seen a goose in years. They'd wake me up at night honking from May onward when they were nesting. Then the goslings would come, and coyotes, too, sometimes, at night. One goose would squawk to warn the others and they'd all circle the goslings and squawk together. We might have learned something from them.

—That we might, I said. Then it dawned on me. You're thinking about starting a new church.

He laughed a little, as though despite himself.

—No, not exactly. A church, yes. But more than that: a school. Not right on the lake but halfway. A school and a church. We have to teach, Azalea. You know it better than anyone, and he gestured around the room theatrically. It isn't enough just to survive. There has to be a reason. There has to be a path into the future.

—Yes, I said, and shifted an empty stapler on the counter. Yes.

—Don't think it's for me, Azalea. Not me alone. But you know, I'm the oldest person I know and I want to do some good while I can.

I gave up the last of my anger. I sent it down the ramp to stroke Black Locust's fur.

—More people go to church than to the market, Joe. More even than come here, most days.

—Business has never been better it's true, he said drily. And I don't even keep a plate anymore. But hope is a dime too. There's something better out there. There has to be.

Outside, Jeff Tanner's voice and buzzy mandolin lifted in joyful lament:

He'd glide cross the floor with the girl he adored
And the band played on.
But his brain was so loaded it nearly exploded
The poor girl would shake with alarm.
He'd ne'er leave the girl with the strawberry curls
And the band played on.

—Don't you ever wonder why it happened, Azalea? You probably hardly remember. You were just a little girl.

—I remember everything, I said. What I don't remember Daniel remembers for me.

—Yes. Daniel. Where is he now?

I said nothing.

—Look, he said. I'm not asking you to pull up stakes. It's just halfway. And lots of things need shuttling back and forth all the time: medical supplies, generators, fuel, spare parts, clothes, canned food, toothbrushes. A million things. We've done well here but no one's making batteries out of birch bark.

—They're making aspirin out of willow though. *Salix alba.*

—I've had more than one request for the LCBO, too. I never thought pastoral service would extend to looting liquor stores but here we are.

—It's not looting.

—I know.

—There's a building of sorts. It isn't much but it's standing and has power, or will. And you don't have to decide right away. There's others that could do it but it should be you. You know it and I know it or I wouldn't be here.

I looked outside, through the whole high bank of windows facing the parking lot. I tried to comprehend it all: the market, people milling, the surrounding lawn and the community garden, the orchard. My parents. They had been in Toronto, along with the professor's wife. I saw an absence spread like a cloud along the prevailing westerlies over cities in mourning: Toronto, Ajax, Whitby, Oshawa. And farther off the unimaginable: Chicago, New York, Detroit, Kansas City, Denver. Alamogordo. Names in a pantheon, lost as Atlantis.

—I have to talk to Daniel, I said.

—Of course. I want you to be sure.

I left the counter and walked quickly toward the stairs.

A is for Azalea

I have never been in a hospital but I know about them. They have pale green hallways and neon lights, and the beds are metal and surrounded by heavy beige curtains, and there's an antiseptic smell. Machines whirr and beep and keep your blood clean and give you air if you can't breathe on your own. Doctors and nurses bustle around in white clothes. People go there when they're sick. We don't have a hospital in Welcome but Daniel has me. I wasn't there to help him live but to help him.

I smoothed the hair out of his eyes. He seemed to be reviving, though I knew better and he did, too. He closed his eyes for a long while, and when he opened them a veil had fallen, the first. I had seen this before. Everyone has.

—I see them you know. I see them all the time.

—Who, Daniel?

— Our families. My parents and yours and my sister.

—You have a sister? You never told me that. What's her name?

155

—I did. I do. Cass. Cassie. Cassandra. Cassiopeia was the joke. Cassidy when she was a teenager. She was two years younger than me. She lived in Denver.

He coughed and reached toward the night table.
—Here.
—Thanks.

He drank, coughed, then coughed again in a hard wracking fit. He reached for the glass again and his hand shook. Another veil.
—Your father was a friend of my parents when I was a kid. I know you know that. They were at the base, my father underground and yours above. I liked him: he gave me my first bicycle, which you inherited. They'd drop by Christmases before you were born. I moved to live with my aunt, then here. Malmstrom. Warren. Denver. I was with her though, Cass. I was there. I saw my arm. You don't believe me. I can still see the house. Curtains blowing like a black and white movie. Nothing outside. Nothing inside.
—You loved your sister and that's how you remember her. I dream about my parents all the time.
—She shouldn't have been alone.
—Maybe she wasn't.

The room was getting dark. The power had been turned off for the night so I went to the kitchen for a candle. There were no good ones, just lumps on the piano in the living room, but I saw that Daniel had left a fully fueled oil lamp—an old-fashioned farmhouse lamp with a wick and tall chimney—sitting on the kitchen counter next to a box of matches. I wondered why he hadn't taken it with him up to his room. Then I understood. I lit the lamp.

He had changed again and seemed afloat in a hazy blue light coming in from the window. I touched his chest and he opened his eyes without seeing. The final veil.
—Three days they said. I promised. We did the best we could, Nora and me. How could I know we were never really here? I'm sorry.

I leaned forward until my face was over his. My sudden tears fell onto his cheeks.

—Daniel? Daniel, can you see them? Daniel?

I was still leaning over him when Bailey came bounding into the room. He jumped up to lick my face and went scrambling into every corner, looking for water.

B is for Beginning

I have been keeping a diary of sorts—or tending, rather, as one tends a garden. Yet a garden makes a gardener out of the librarian one used to be, and after a time one may easily picture oneself standing beside a contusion of hyacinth and poppies like a statue of Guanyin pouring out her vase, the garden like a sleeve upon one's marble skin scabrous with mildew, staring from the dirt of one's chiseled eye-pits. So it has lately appeared, though admittedly one has lately also set aside individual will as one sets aside shears after trimming a box hedge for a parterre. In this view, however, one cannot be certain whether the garden has not already employed those same subtle shears by which the librarian first became a gardener. Thus tending one is tended, and the diary grows.

I have taken lately to lying among the wild grasses and sedge near the shore of the pond. Nobody cuts there anymore and the wild rye (*Elymus canadensis*) and *Poaceae* and *Bromus* grow unchecked. The awns of the rye, my favourite, hang pendulous as snakeskin and rattle out their Latin upon the wind. It's both too early and too late for grasshoppers, so I lie on my belly with my chin on my stacked fists and watch the heads of rye dangle and sway in the summer breeze. After a few minutes of silence, as if to gauge my sincerity, the papery whisper of the rye slithers toward me out of the air and earth: *Lorem ipsum dolor* they start in a reedy hiss, then *E Pluribus*

Unum a little more firmly, and *Carthago deleta est*, and finally a bold *veni vidi fugi*. Ha ha I say out of politeness. *Seize the day* they answer in plain English to let me know it's alright.

In the beginning, they tell me, the earth was without form and void. Then the twins Spartina and Andropogon, the titan angiosperm, descended from heaven to seed the first monocots on the wild verge of Baxter Creek. Men dammed the creek with logs to gather its power, and the creek widened into a pond. A saw mill appeared and burned; a flour mill; a paper mill; a distillery. A spur of the national railroad stretched out. The dam became concrete and the wild verge collected bulrushes, jewel weed, sweet gale, and willow. A town rose below the dam. Mowers came, the dreadful, and the rye was pinned against the bulrushes at the pond's edge—like a boxer they tell me. Suddenly the mowers vanished. This, the rye says, nodding, this was the grace of the twins returning at need to safeguard the faithful. Depend upon it, they say. Besides, how else do you explain the pond's ideal proportions, the wild verge, its perfect soil, the precise balance of lignin and saccharides in their own exemplary bodies—engineered, they proclaim over the grumbling fescue, planned, to endure the otherwise unsurvivable westerlies? *Listen to the light* they tell me; *see the wind.*

I stand up and brush myself off, then start climbing back up the hill toward the library. The sun is setting straight down the empty highway behind me and the diminishing glow lifts my shadow. No one can follow me now, no one with a name at least, and between the swing sets and the cemetery of the founders I close my eyes and try once again to forget my own, though I am tangled in its meridians.

In the beginning there was no beginning and the void was without either form or earth. Then I moved to Welcome. No: I was married first. I was married and then the mowers came, the dreadful, and Daniel who is everywhere.

The earth coalesced in tumbling space over millions of years. An explosion, a ripple, a ball and a spinning disk; the ball ignites and the disk blooms; the titans recede. A broiling planet cools, is shattered in a collision, burns and cools again. Water collects and covers the surface. In a fumarole in the deep ocean an ion gradient appears in pores of green Serpentinite. A proton finds a neutron and a flicker takes hold. Single-celled microbes, archaea, stain the ocean purple and poison the atmosphere with oxygen. The planet freezes, thaws, turns green, freezes again. It is the Proterozoic. The global ocean precipitates iron for a billion years, folding it on the seabed in undulating bands of red and black. It is the Cambrian: life crawls up, then death. Volcanoes erupt and continents move: Columbia, Rodinia, Gondwana, Pangaea. Manhattan scrapes Africa; India is adrift; Siberia is a jungle. A rock falls and the dinosaurs vanish; mammals walk under different trees with babies on their hips. Welcome emerges from a shallow inland sea and Baxter Creek flows and men dam it with logs to harness its power. A pond forms. A town rises. Mowers come, the dreadful. The earth burns. The twins do not appear, yet Welcome is, nevertheless, one must concede, preserved largely intact. I begin collecting patches for a quilt.

About the Author

Dennis Vanderspek lives by a pond with his wife and dogs. This is his first novel.

A Checklist of JEF Titles

www.ingramcontent.com/pod-product-compliance
Lightning Source LLC
Chambersburg PA
CBHW030508260626
47157CB00005B/1701